Unexpected Pleasure

Dara Girard

ILORI
Press Books, LLC

Unexpected Pleasure

ILORI PRESS BOOKS, LLC
13217 New Hampshire Avenue, #10332
Silver Spring, MD 20904
www.iloripressbooks.com

Other Books by Dara

The Black Stockings Society

Power Play
A Gentleman's Offer
Body Chemistry

Return of the Black Stockings Society

Playing for Keeps
After Hours
A Private Affair
Just One Look

Henson Series

Table for Two
Gaining Interest
Careless Rapture
Dangerous Curves
Familiar Stranger

The Clifton Sisters

The Sapphire Pendant
The Amber Stone

Dear Reader,

The idea for the series *It Happened One Wedding* came to me out of nowhere. I was finishing up my book *Just One Look*, a story about a woman who meets the man she left standing at the altar, when another idea popped in my head.

What if a woman got dumped at her sister's wedding?

The 'what if' question is a storyteller's goldmine and before I knew it I had sketched out that story and two others—enough for a series. I found the wedding setting intriguing because it's filled with emotion and I wanted to put a spin on a commonly used formula. Most romance novels end with a wedding, but as some couples know, weddings are just the beginning…

I hope you enjoy *Unexpected Pleasure.*

All the best,
Dara

You can find out more about this series and learn about my other titles on my web site, www.daragirard.com.

Chapter One

"**I** don't love you anymore."

Sticks and stones...

"I know I should have told you this earlier."

May break my bones...

"I thought I could ignore how I feel."

But words will never hurt me.

"I'm so sorry."

Doran Gibson stared into the beautiful brown eyes of Megan Thurman, the woman who'd just taken a bite out of his heart and spat it on the ground. He tried his best to calculate what his next move should be. He shifted his gaze to one of the large castle windows where his reflection looked back at him. Funny, he didn't look like a monster. He looked very ordinary—a well dressed black man in a dark suit, behind him the lush English countryside showing off all its spring greenery as dusk slowly settled over it.

He could hear the gentle murmur of other guests and the soft gurgle of a brook where guests could go fishing, wind its way gently through the landscape a few yards away. No, he didn't look like a monster, although he felt like one. Because no ordinary man would want to lift the glass table—fine china, white wine filled glasses, red umbrella and all—and smash it to the ground and stomp on it with such force that Megan would scream.

And he wanted to hear her scream with bloodcurdling intensity just like in a horror movie, her eyes round as headlights in her perfect oval face. No, an ordinary man wouldn't dream of doing something so destructive. Only a monster would want to grab his chair and fling it towards the brook and let his shout of rage mingle with screams of terror. An ordinary man would just…he wasn't sure yet.

"I just couldn't come to the meeting alone," Megan continued, her voice low and full of regret.

He had flown with her to England to attend a meeting, where he'd helped her family business secure a major German supplier for half of the cost they usually charged.

"I didn't mean anything more by it."

Sticks and stones…

She sighed, licking her rose colored lips, her blue blouse rising and falling with each breath. Blue was his favorite color. He'd thought she'd worn the blouse especially for him. He'd been an idiot. "Doran, are you listening?"

May break my bones. But words will never hurt me.

"Doran, this is important."

Lies. Lies. All lies. Words could hurt. Did hurt. They hurt so much that the air seemed to claw at his face, the slightest breeze felt like a band-aid ripping the hairs from his arm. She didn't love him. She didn't love him anymore. Maybe never had loved him. And she was sorry. Sorry for giving him hope. Was she also sorry for making him love her? For taking a year out of his life? A woman like her was use to men falling at her feet. Not only was she gorgeous and from an established family, she was kind and funny and…damn. He didn't want to remember how wonderful she was. He wanted to hate her right now, but couldn't.

How could he blame her for what he felt? Wasn't he the fool? Wasn't he the one dumb enough to fall in love all by himself? A year wasn't a lifetime. He snapped the red necklace box closed. A futile act since she'd already rejected what was inside: A necklace he'd had designed specifically for her, the one he imagined would complement the family ring he'd planned to give her when he asked her to marry him.

"Doran, please say something."

She lightly touched his hand. She had no right to touch him. She could pity him, but touching him was crossing the line. He didn't pull his hand back, but his dark gaze gave her warning and she quickly snatched her hand back realizing her error.

He was only here in this fourteenth century castle because of her. Because she'd told him how important coming to this meeting was. How much meeting with the UK branch was essential to her success. She wanted to be promoted to a key position in her father's company and needed his help in a business that was struggling against their more well-positioned competitors. He'd even paid for all the expenses, because he knew her family's company was on shaky ground, but had not minded. He'd always enjoyed supporting her and only this morning, in a boardroom, he'd done just that. He'd even dressed up to take her to her favorite theater, he should have suspected her silence throughout the show meant something was wrong. Now with the deal sealed and them alone in the castle dining area, she didn't need him anymore.

"Doran please. Just say something. Even if it's one word."

What the hell did she want him to say? That it was okay? That he understood? Did she want him to reassure her? He wouldn't give her that pleasure. That was the only power he had left.

He shoved his chair back.

Megan quickly glanced around. "Please don't make a scene."

Doran narrowed his gaze and she had the grace to look embarrassed. She should have known better, he wasn't the type. He tucked the necklace box inside his jacket pocket. He'd hoped to surprise her, he'd been the one surprised instead. Now he didn't know what to do with himself. He stood and turned.

Seconds later he felt her hand on his arm and winced as if she'd slapped him. She snatched her hand back, but held his gaze. "Doran," she said in a soft plea. "I'm really sorry."

There were a lot of things he wanted to say, but his tongue wouldn't move, his throat felt tight and he could feel the stinging of tears behind his eyes. No, he wouldn't say anything because there was nothing to say.

He turned.

"Please don't tell—"

He spun around, halting her words. The note in her voice was new, the pleading was replaced by something different. Something he could use—fear. He knew what she was asking him and he'd comply. He just wouldn't let her know that. Let her be a little nervous, anxious, worried. He lifted a brow, flashed a brief grin and walked away.

Doran changed his flight to an earlier return then aimlessly walked the grounds. Walking around the castle as if he were a sentinel on guard. After doing that for nearly a half hour he went inside and headed up the main staircase and down the red carpeted hallway to his room. He turned a corner then stopped when he saw Megan in front of one of the doors. He couldn't tell if she was coming or going. He'd wait until she left. He didn't want to see her right now, he'd walk another half hour around the castle if he had to. He turned to head back downstairs.

"Darling, I'm sorry."

He spun around at the sound of her voice. His heart lifted. Had it all been a mistake? Had she felt that she'd acted too hasty? He returned to the hall and saw a man standing in the doorway. Doran's heart turned cold when he recognized the face: Adam Holbrooke, her father's lawyer. A tall black man with a trim beard and boyishly handsome features who'd risen more by connection than intelligence. He'd been at the meeting–silent as the puppet he was— letting Doran negotiate most of the deal.

He'd never suspected anything between them.

"I'm sorry I kept you waiting," she said.

Doran watched them embrace, acid burning in his stomach.

"How did he take it?" Adam asked, his arms wrapped loosely around her waist.

"Better than expected."

"I didn't think this would work. He didn't seem the type and they were a hard group."

"I told you Doran is smarter than he seems. His mother has no idea, but I could see it. You were worried for no reason."

"If we didn't make this deal happen your father was go- ing to fire me, and my father would have served my ass on a platter."

She patted his backside and with a smile said, "You have a nice one."

"So do you."

They kissed then she pulled away and said, "Now we don't have to worry about anything."

"But what if—?"

She pressed a finger to his lips. "No one is going to ask any questions, you're the main contact now. All correspondence will go through you so you can take the credit for this."

Adam shook his head. "I don't know. We should give this some time."

"I want to be with you, I can't stand pretending to ignore Doran's little…" She paused as if searching for words. "Eccentricities," she finished. "Especially when he's upset. It's better this way. There's no more time to waste. Doran is not the kind to cause trouble. He'll lick his wounds and disappear. He won't mention this meeting. He's too proud."

"You'd better hope so."

"I know it." She smiled. "I know my men."

"We're just little boys to you, aren't we?" he said with affection.

"Yes, and I have my favorites." She kissed him.

Doran turned away, though the image remained in his mind. Adam and Megan? They'd planned this? They were having an affair? She'd used him to get a deal so that her lover could take the credit?

She couldn't stand his eccentricities? Doran rested his head against the wall. He didn't know what hurt more—a broken heart or the sense of betrayal.

He's too proud. Maybe he shouldn't be. Maybe he should confront her and let her know what he thought, maybe he should call her father up and tell him who had really negotiated the deal. Who cared if it made him look pathetic?

He sighed. He did. He didn't like being a fool and he didn't want anyone else to know it. Plus, telling her father would only reveal what he'd tried to hide for years. How smart he was. He'd played on his carefree, easy-going persona for years and it had worked for him so far and he planned to let it work for years to come. He'd cultivated it out of necessity—he'd learned early that nothing could please his mother so he quickly stopped trying. His brother paid the price of being the smart one, running the company that he planned to give to his son one day. He took his older brother role seriously leaving Doran free to be his mother's favorite disappointment.

"If only you'd apply yourself more," she'd say whenever she saw his report card. He did his barest minimum for the company and had broken free seven years ago at age twenty-seven. Not even his siblings knew how quickly he could crunch numbers or that he could assess a situation and see nuances most people missed. When he'd noticed the pizzeria chain his family had sold to a larger conglomerate was back on the market, he'd casually discussed it with his brother, until his brother thought buying the company back was his idea.

Doran didn't mind not getting the credit. He hadn't liked seeing how the corporate culture was affecting the workers or the reputation of a business his grandfather had taken over fifty years ago. He'd bought one struggling pizza place and with drive and ambition, Mamma Tolino's Pizza had expanded into several outlets along the East Coast. Two new acquisitions, of smaller pizzerias that were folded into the Mamma Tolino brand, had been his idea, and he'd quietly arranged for certain favorable clauses in the contracts that made sure their workforce had one of the highest retention and loyalty rate in the region, but again, he'd given his sister credit for the idea and had learned it was easier to let others think he was stupid. No responsibility, no expectations, no disappointment.

But he'd blown his cover for Megan. Because he'd loved her, because he'd wanted the best for her. He'd planned a future with her. And she'd played him. She knew he wouldn't tell anyone, not just because of pride, but because of what it would cost him.

He'd already bowed to the pressure to get married. He'd only looked in Megan's direction because of his mother's insistence and he'd fallen hard. He'd been ready to put his carefree life behind him. But not anymore. His mother could nag him, be disappointed with him, but he wouldn't fall prey to his heart or sense of duty again. If he died a bachelor, so what? If his mother thought he was a reckless playboy, he didn't care. He wouldn't be made a fool of again.

Doran took a deep breath. Fine. He'd miscalculated. He wouldn't do it again. He glanced at Adam and Megan framed in the arched castle window down the hall, making them appear like newlyweds headed to their bridal suite, before they disappeared into the room.

Doran shoved his hands in his pockets and said in a low voice, "I'll let this go, but you'd better hope we don't meet again."

Chapter Two

Tanna Ariyo didn't have a limitless bank account to pay for her deception. Graham Black, the man she'd hired to pretend to be her boyfriend for her twin sisters' double wedding, was the best her money could buy.

Perhaps if she'd paid more, he wouldn't have gotten tipsy and hit on one of the bridesmaids. Tanna sat stoically among the scent of jollof rice and baked plantain as imported palm wine flowed along with the white and red variety. The white of the large cowrie shell centerpieces, representing fertility and prosperity in the Yoruba tradition of Nigeria, caught the light of the expansive chandeliers overhead in the castle ballroom. The brides and grooms had already gone through most of the celebration before her humiliation. Ironically it happened soon after the ritual of tasting the four elements: Lemon, vinegar, cayenne and honey.

The lemon signifying sour feelings, the vinegar bitter experiences, cayenne for hot moments and honey for sweet, wrapping everything up. Life was like that, but right now Tanna felt as if her life was a gallon of vinegar and there was nothing to remedy that. She'd spent—wasted—money so that Graham would make her look good.

So that she didn't have to attend Feyi and Fola's destination wedding alone. Everyone already felt bad that her younger sisters—yes *both* of them, they always liked to add in whispers—had married before her, and she'd despaired of having to endure another long evening of pitying stares. She'd thought of coming up with an excuse like the flu or malaria, but nothing seemed to work. Her sisters wanted her there and her absence would have been noticed.

"You have to go," her mother had said when Tanna had brought up the idea. "Not showing up will be just as pathetic as going alone." They sat in the family house in suburban Maryland as her mother added even more names to a guest list that could rival Father Christmas'. Although the wedding would be in England, where a number of their relatives lived, it would also be broadcast online to Nigeria, Brazil, Canada and America. So her single status could be broadcast across continents.

"So you see me as pathetic?" Tanna asked, trying to appear nonchalant, although it was difficult to have a serious conversation with her mother while her seventy-nine year old grandmother sang in the kitchen as she cut up red peppers, her words partly in English, Yoruba and another language all her own, when she forgot the lyrics.

"No," her mother said quickly. "Just unfortunate. If only…"

"If only what?" Tanna prodded, although she didn't

really need to ask. Everyone felt they knew the exact reason why she was still unmarried.

"You're too picky."

"You're too heavy."

"You're not heavy enough."

"You're too smart."

Some even dared to suggest that she was too dark, though her father thought that was nonsense, calling her his sweet little blackberry.

But it didn't matter. Most people blamed her for her single status.

Always too-too something, although no one would admit that she wasn't as heavy as her cousin Lola who'd gotten married last spring. Or as smart as her friend Nadine who'd married three years ago.

So she came up with a plan. She'd invent a boyfriend for the event and then break up a month after. As a professional house stager, she was very aware of the importance of presentation. She considered every detail. She'd contacted a local agency, Escort For You, that assured her they were legitimate, exclusive and discreet. Their motto was: *Why go alone when you can just pick up the phone?* She hadn't called, preferring to make her arrangements online, but had been impressed with their history and extensive vetting.

The fact that her hired date was British wouldn't be a problem so no one would suspect anything, and made all the plans. Two days, all expenses paid. All he had to do was dote on her and make her look desirable.

Three months before the wedding, she'd started her sham, hinting at the new man in her life. Since she had yet to meet someone, she kept as much as she could vague. She was glad she did. By the time the wedding day arrived everyone was eager to meet him and when he'd arrived she'd been eager to show him off. And he'd been worth showing off. Cultured, funny, attractive. Until he started to drink.

Obviously he'd never tasted palm wine before and had a preference for it. She didn't know how many glasses he'd had before he'd publicly dumped her and gone for one of her cousins. It didn't matter which one, she had so many she could fill a small university with them. She just knew it was one of the younger, flashier ones with big hips and bright lipstick.

She tapped the stem of her wine glass as she watched them dancing together for everyone to see.

"Sista, no worries," a family friend said in passing to comfort her. "He is no good."

Tanna plastered on a smile. "I'm not much of a dancer and he likes to have fun."

But the family friend saw through her lie and walked away. Moments later she sat with two other older women wearing elaborate pink lace outfits who sent glances in her direction as if they were nurses looking at a patient who was terminal.

Tanna drummed her fingers on the table. It would have been better if she'd come alone. She'd wanted to avoid pity, instead she was getting it in spades.

She was sick of pity. Sick of the 'oh poor Tanna' looks. "Oh poor Tanna having to see her younger sisters married before her." "Oh poor Tanna dumped at their wedding by a man who we all knew was just too good to be true. He was just too pretty to be decent." "No, it's because he's white, she doesn't know how to read white men." "Did she really think she could fool us?"

A woman pulled out a chair beside her and sat down. It was her Aunt Violet, a woman Tanna and her sisters secretly called Aunt Violence because she had a wicked way of making a point. She was a stately woman of measured tones—she never yelled or whispered—but her words always had an impact. Like Tanna, she wore the red and gold *aso-ebi*, the outfit made from the same matching fabric and pattern to denote the unity and support of the bride's family. While Tanna's dress sported a crushed red velvet bodice that flowed to a mermaid style skirt, her aunt's dress was completely gold with a splash of red lace and on her head a golden colored *gele* so big and wide it looked like it could block out the sun. She was of medium height, but sat as if she were much taller and half expected four men to come lift her chair and carry it to wherever she directed them.

"You should have made sure he was black," she said.

Tanna watched Graham move in beautiful rhythm with her cousin. "I don't know what you mean."

"How much did he cost you?"

Tanna shook her head. "Nope, I still don't know what you mean."

"You told us he was brown skinned."

"I don't remember being particular."

And she hadn't been race specific, although she had requested the agency get her a black man. Unfortunately, her first choice had gotten sick and Graham had been his replacement. She should have cancelled.

"I suppose it doesn't matter what race he is," Aunt Violet allowed, smoothing out a crease in the tablecloth. "Only what he is not. Your boyfriend. The man you've been seeing these last three months."

"I was seeing someone."

"Then why not just tell us he couldn't make it, instead of this ridiculous sham of yours?"

Tanna shrugged, her stoic mask back in place. She hoped if she looked like she didn't care her aunt would leave her alone. "I don't know."

"You've been staging homes too long, you're confusing what really matters to what people think should matter."

Tanna folded her arms. She was used to the criticism of her career choice. She hadn't continued the family tradition of going into law or the sciences. She felt a sharp pinch in her side. "Ow!" she turned and saw her aunt putting the butter knife back on the table. She rubbed her side. "What was that for?"

"That expression on your face."

"What expression?"

"You think feeling sorry for yourself will change anything? You think sending angry glances to that man will make him come to you? Are you practicing witchcraft?"

"No."

"Then do something."

"What am I supposed to do?"

"Anything, but sit here like a pile of pounded yam. Dance, talk, eat. Have a good time without him. Even when the wind slaps your face you must hold your head high."

"But I don't…all right, all right," she said quickly when her aunt reached for the butter knife again.

"You are an Ariyo. And what does that mean?"

"We always keep our back straight no matter the burden," she said, repeating a familiar phrase. Yes, she'd been taught not to show her emotions, to weather any storm, to face failure with a smile. But sometimes she just wanted to fall apart and cry.

"Good," Aunt Violet said pleased, lifting Tanna's chin. "Now why would such a pretty woman curse her sisters' wedding with such a sour expression? Smile. No, not like that. Are you trying to be funny? Yes, like that. Much better. And keep that smile until the night is over. You can let it fall when the night is through." She stood then pointed at Tanna. "And until then it better not go missing."

Tanna kept her smile in place and nodded.

The moment her aunt turned she let her smile fall. She could pretend, but not that much. She'd prefer to look stoic rather than like a child high on sweets.

Her aunt turned around and glared at her.

Tanna put the smile back in place. She'd rather be humiliated than catch her aunt's wrath. Her aunt was right; she didn't want to ruin her sisters' special day. She didn't want everyone remembering that she'd been dumped by some British man who could move well on the dance floor.

She'd get her refund later. Tomorrow she'd tell Escort For You what she thought of their services, but for now she had to endure the evening—with a smile.

However, after an hour of smiling, Tanna felt as if her face would fall off. She feigned laughter and cheer until her energy wore thin. Her date had disappeared from the dance floor and she hadn't seen him, but she hadn't seen her cousin either and could only imagine where they were making their next dance moves. The castle had fifteen cottages where guests could stay. She didn't want to imagine how they would use them.

She needed to escape. She needed fresh air. Tanna excused herself from a group discussing the kind of lace they needed to buy for another upcoming wedding and headed for the back doorway, but her aunt caught her before she could make her getaway.

Chapter Three

"Where are you going?"

Tanna paused then slowly turned, making sure her smile was firmly in place. "I'm going for a smoke."

"You don't smoke."

"I'm thinking of starting."

Her aunt continued to stare at her, finding no amusement in her joke.

Tanna briefly glanced around the crowded ballroom to see who she could use as an excuse to distract her. She spotted a man who was distinguished looking with a military stance and likely the age of her grandfather, she'd spoken to him before and nearly wept with boredom as he gave her a detailed account of the ten days he'd spent in Japan, twenty years ago. He wouldn't work as a diversion.

She switched her gaze to another man with pepper grey hair and a trim goatee who seemed like a possibility, but when she briefly met his gaze he actually licked his lips. She immediately broke eye contact. She was desperate, but not that desperate. "I won't be gone long."

"I have someone I want you to meet. She has a son."

Four dangerous words. A hungry matchmaking mother at a wedding was a tenacious creature, she had to escape now. She inched towards the door. "Just a minute. My smile is slipping."

"Good, as long as it doesn't fall you're fine," she said, clapping her hand around Tanna's wrist with the intensity of handcuffs. "Now come on."

"Aunty please."

"He's a doctor."

"Aren't they all?" she mumbled.

"What was that?"

"I mean wouldn't it be funny if you said he was a mechanic or photographer? That would be a change."

Her aunt blinked, making it clear she didn't think it would be funny at all.

Tanna shook her head and sighed. "Never mind."

"Let's go."

Tanna's struggled to pull her hand free. "I just have to use the toilet."

Her aunt sighed. "Fine. Don't make me wait too long though."

"I won't."

Her aunt stared at her for a long moment, then nodded and released her hold. "Very well."

Freedom at last. Tanna made a dash to the large wooden doors heading out of the ballroom, then promptly halted when her mother blocked her path. "Your aunt may have a man for you," she said. Getting past her mother would be impossible. She was a tall, big boned woman with fine features and naturally long lashes she played up today with glitter.

"Mum, please not now."

"The man you brought was rubbish, never mind him. This chance—"

Tanna moved to the side. "I'll be back."

Her mother did the same. "But where are you going?"

"Slowly insane."

Her mother blinked.

"Get it?" Tanna said with a grin. "You asked me where I was going and I said I'm *going* slowly insane. It's a joke."

Her mother patted Tanna's upper arm and stared at her as if she were a wayward child. "My darling, how many times have I told you that you're not funny?"

"Clearly not enough to stop me from trying."

"Come."

Tanna jumped back before her mother could grab her. Getting her aunt to release her would be a lot easier than her mother. "I just need a few minutes and I'll be right back. I promise."

Her mother made a grab for her again. Tanna stepped back and folded her arms. "I have to use the toilet."

"At times like this you can hold your bladder. Opportunities are to be seized," her mother said, making the motion of grabbing something with both hands. "And held on tight."

"Yes, I know."

"Otherwise someone else can get it."

"I know that too."

"The Davises have a single daughter younger than you and—"

"If I make a tiny puddle in the middle of the room, I think my chances for a prospective husband will plummet anyway."

Her mother frowned. "You really have to go?"

"Yes."

Mrs. Ariyo gestured to the door. "Go then, and remember—"

"I'll be right back." Tanna kissed her mother on the cheek to soften her interruption then hurried away. She was a foot from the door when two identically beautiful women dressed in white jumped in front of her with worried eyes.

"Don't cry," her sister Fola said.

Her other sister Feyi added, "He doesn't deserve you."

"I'm not going to cry," Tanna said, feeling tears of frustration build up behind her eyes. Were the stars against her? Would she never escape this room?

Fola touched her hand. "It probably would have been better..."

"If you'd come alone," Feyi finished. She always finished her sister's sentences at times like this.

"We hope you don't think..."

"You ever need to prove anything to us."

"We love you..."

"No matter what."

"I know that," Tanna said. "And you don't have to worry about me. I am okay. Really. Truly. Absolutely. I just need to use the facilities."

Fola touched Tanna's hand. "To cry in private."

"We understand," Feyi said, patting her arm.

She wouldn't correct them. It wouldn't matter anyway. She nodded then hurried to the door, breathing a sigh of relief when she finally reached it. She pumped her fist in triumph and headed outside, leaving the castle ballroom behind her. Tanna walked around the side of the castle then stopped when she saw a man standing alone, staring out at the landscape.

Chapter Four

He met her three favorite possibilities in a man. All beginning with B. He was big, bald and brown. He wore an expensive suit, his face had an angular jawline framed by dark eyebrows. He looked a little mean, but perhaps that was just his resting face. As a house stager she'd learned how to assess situations—show her any house and she could make it sellable—quickly, and make them look just the way she wanted them to. Was he another guest who'd come outside to get space? She didn't want to go back anytime soon and he would make a good excuse.

She walked over to him, wine and humiliation giving her a boldness she'd never had before. She didn't care about being turned down. If it had been two days ago she wouldn't have dared, even just an hour ago a man like him would have intimidated her, but she felt too low in spirit to care. Maybe he'd even be rude and she could get into an argument—a little verbal sparring could be fun.

She walked over to him. "You look like you've had a bad day, how about I get you a drink?"

He turned to her and she took a step back. She'd underestimated him. From a distance he'd looked mean, but up close. Up close he was another major B—beautiful. She'd never seen such perfect, stunning features on a man before and his dark eyes met hers with an intensity that caused her heart to race. No, she'd chosen the wrong target. He probably wasn't even human. Heaven had lost one of its angels. Maybe he'd laugh at her. That would be okay, at least she'd make someone laugh today.

He shoved his hands in his pockets. "Sure."

She nodded with quick acceptance and a nervous laugh. "That's what I thought you'd say. Sorry to bother you." Tanna turned and headed back inside. She didn't want to go back, but aimlessly roaming around would just be sad. She was a few yards away from the entrance when she felt a presence beside her. She stopped and turned and saw the man, his hands in his pockets his gaze on the ground. "Are you following me?"

He glanced up surprised. "Yes."
"Why?"

He furrowed his brows and tilted his head to the side as if she puzzled him. "Because you offered me a drink and I said sure."

She blinked. He'd said 'sure'? How come she hadn't heard that? What was going on? This beautiful man had actually said yes? Maybe he thought she was offering a lot more than a drink. She'd deal with that later. She'd just let him know that she kept a knife underneath her *gele*. That lie had worked once before with an over amorous man at another party. For now she'd reassess the situation. Clearly he wasn't an angel—unless he was an angel who liked free drinks—and he wasn't British, which was fine. He had a nice, deep voice and an accent that sounded from the Northeastern part of America. His stance showed he was a man in full control of himself, but she still sensed he was upset about something. Not her problem. He had said yes, don't question too much. She imagined her mother grasping the air and saying, "Seize the opportunity."

And she would. She was going to treat this man to a drink and enjoy every moment. She looped her arm through his, his forearm was as big and tight as coiled steel. "Come on then," she said, faking a tone of nonchalance as her mind raced. What was she doing and why was he letting her? "We'll head back into the lion's den."

"Lion's den?"

"The castle ballroom."

"You're with the wedding party?"

"Yes." She paused. "You're not?"

"No."

She looked at his suit again, it looked too styled to be for ordinary business. "You just came from one?"

"A wedding?"

"No, I'm sorry, a party."

"Something like that. Will what I'm wearing be a problem?"

"No," she said with a wave of her hand, hoping he didn't see it tremble. Even if there had been a problem, she'd find a way to make it disappear. "Fortunately, there are so many people no one will notice. Just follow my lead and you'll be fine."

Minutes later, the two of them sat at the bar with red wine for her, beer for him. She'd conveniently situated them towards the back so that she could hide from her mother and aunt.

"Why are you offering strangers a drink?" he asked.

"If you're nervous that you'll be thrown out, don't be. My parents are footing the bill for this little soiree. This is my twin sisters' wedding. Both of them are getting married on the same day. For the rest of my life I'll have to do double anniversary cards as well as birthdays. They'll both probably schedule to get pregnant at the same time as well, which is fine. I love them. I'm happy for them. But tonight I'm trying my best not to be known as the sister whose date ended up with one of the bridesmaids."

He lifted a brow. "Seriously?"

"I know. How cliché is that? Flirting with a bridesmaid. It would have been more interesting if he'd gone for a groomsmen."

The man choked on his drink. "You would have preferred it?"

She thought for a moment. "Not personally, but it would have made a more lively story in the retelling. A man leaving you for your younger, pretty cousin is just sad."

"Where is she?"

"Why? You want to make a comparison yourself?"

The man looked at Tanna for a long moment, his dark penetrating eyes seeming to take in every inch of her, making her skin tingle. "Something like that."

She swallowed. She wasn't sure what just happened, but she liked it. Was he actually flirting with her? How many drinks had he had? She shook her head and looked out at the dance floor. "She's not here and neither is he."

His brows shot up. "They left together?"

She nodded then giggled and leaned towards him. "But do you want to know what makes it worse?" she said in a low voice.

The man leaned forward too, giving her a whiff of his cologne. Or did he just smell that good naturally? Too bad a man like him hadn't been available at Escort for You. If only…she glanced down when she felt a hand on her arm.

"You zoned out on me," he said, pulling his hand away.

"I'm sorry."

"You were about to tell me what's worse."

"Oh yes, right." She had to focus. She didn't want to ruin this night by having him think she was nuts. He was probably use to women fawning all over him. She cleared her throat ready to share her embarrassment. "The worst part is that I hired him."

"To do what?"

"To be my date for the evening."

"Wait, so the guy you hired—"

She quickly covered his mouth. "Shh! Don't talk so loud."

He removed her hand and lowered his voice, although he sounded no less stunned. "The guy you hired to be your date dumped you and ran off with your cousin?"

"Yes, but that's our secret, okay? I've been pretending for the last three months that I have a boyfriend so that's what my family will think happened."

He furrowed his brows. "They'll think what happened?"

"That my boyfriend dumped me."

"But you don't have a boyfriend."

"No, just the one I hired. Are you following this?"

"Not very well, but this isn't my first drink of the evening." He finished his glass then set it down.

She nodded towards the empty glass. "Yes, you looked like you've had a hard day too."

"I just found out my girlfriend is having an affair with her father—"

Tanna's eyes widened in horror. "She's having an affair with her father!"

The man sent her a cool, chastising look. "Her father's lawyer. You didn't let me finish."

"I'm sorry," she said, and meant it. His look could make a giraffe feel as big as a beetle.

He wagged his finger at her. "You shouldn't interrupt."

"I'm sorry, go on," she urged, eager to hear the full story.

He shrugged. "There's not much more to say. Megan made a fool of me."

"No, she's the fool for letting you go. That's the best way to think of it."

"A year down the drain."

He looked so sad she wanted to cheer him up. "Do you know how much I spent for that guy?"

"Did you use a local agency?"

She paused. She hadn't expected that question. "Yes."

"How many days did you need him?"

"Two."

"With a set amount of hours each day, correct?"

She nodded wondering where he'd taken the conversation.

"But you had a budget."

She nodded again.

He rubbed his chin then said, "Probably about seven hundred pounds."

Tanna's mouth dropped. "How did you..?"

"So I'm right?" he said, pleased.

"Lucky guess."

"No, let's just say I'm familiar with the practice."

"It was just for a date, nothing more," she clarified in case he thought it was something else.

"Don't worry. I believe you."

"And this," she said pointing to both of them, "is just a drink."

"Pity, I was hoping for more."

"Like what?" she said with a grin, glad to see the sad look on his face had gone. "Something dirty and clichéd?"

He laughed. "Yes."

His face changed when he laughed. He was even better looking, but that wasn't what got her heart racing, he thought she was funny. Or was it the drink? She didn't care. She wanted to make him laugh again. "So did you tell me that sad story so that I'd feel sorry for you and comfort you?"

"Maybe."

"Would you like me to take you far away from here into a private bedroom where only a whisper of silk would separate us?"

He didn't smile. Instead his brows rose a fraction and a second later she knew why when she felt a smack on the back of her head. "What kind of talk is this!" Aunt Violet said.

Tanna spun around. "I was just trying to be funny."

"How many times have we told you that you're not funny?" Aunt Violet nodded to the man. "Who is this man? Who are you?" she demanded of him.

He held out his hand. "I am—"

"Aunty, he's a friend of mine and—"

"You expect me to believe that? Is he another one from the agency? Your Plan Z?"

"You mean Plan B."

"What?"

Tanna waved her hand. "Never mind."

Aunt Violet shot the man a cold look of reproach. "You can go."

"Aunty, I—"

"To speak such filth out in the open like your mouth is a sewer. Have you no shame?"

Tanna looked around as people started to stare to see what the uproar was about, her face burning. She'd finally gotten over one humiliation she didn't want to suffer another one. "Aunty, please lower your voice."

"Didn't I tell you my friend has a son? And you promised you'd come right back."

"I just wanted to—"

Her mother hurried over to them, looking anxious. "What is going on here?"

Aunt Violet scrunched her face as if she'd smelled something foul. "Tanna has invited *another* stranger to pretend to be her man."

"What do you mean by pretend?" her mother asked puzzled.

Tanna shot her aunt a look and for a moment she looked chagrined. "Nothing, Mum," Tanna said. "I was just chatting with this—"

"Stranger," her aunt finished.

"Actually we're not strangers," the man said, taking Tanna's hand. "She's been waiting for me."

Chapter Five

The three women stared at him. Doran didn't mind, he liked the attention and especially the look on the younger woman's face. He never expected to spend the evening with a pretty dark skinned woman with sparkling brown eyes, and temptingly full lips. His day was improving. Megan may have treated him like a fool, but tonight he'd be another woman's hero. He just hoped she'd play along.

"She was waiting for you?" the woman in the large golden colored headwrap said.

"Yes, I surprised her. She didn't expect me to come, so yes, she did hire the other man, but now I'm here. She told me she didn't want to disappoint you, that's why she had the other date."

"You're the one Tanna's been seeing?" the woman with glittered lashes asked.

"The one she's been seeing for three months?" He nodded. "Yes, that's me."

The woman beamed. "Well, then that's wonderful. What is your name?"

"Logan Gibbs," he lied.

"Logan? What does your name mean?"

Doran rubbed the back of his neck. "I don't know."

She pulled out her mobile phone. "Let's find out."

The other woman with the large headwrap covered the screen with her hand. "Never mind, you can look it up later."

"Yes, you're right," she said, tucking the phone away. "What do your parents do?"

"My father has passed, but my mother runs our family business."

"And it's in…?"

"The food industry."

"How large is the business?"

Tanna tugged on her mother's sleeve. "Mum, does it matter?"

"Of course it matters." She turned to him. "Is it small, mid-size or big?"

"Depends. We only pull in several hundred million dollars a year so compared to other national chains we're rather small."

"Excellent." She turned to the other woman with a smile. "Did you hear that, Sista?"

The other woman didn't smile but nodded. "Yes, I heard it."

"We must have your family over for dinner. Let me introduce you to—"

"In a moment," Aunt Violet said, positioning herself between Tanna and her new boyfriend. "I have to say a few words first, if you'll excuse us."

Mrs. Ariyo nodded then left.

Tanna inwardly cringed. She knew her mother leaving wasn't good. Her feeling of unease increased when Aunt Violet loosely clasped her hands together, a gesture that only appeared to be demure.

"I know how to read people," she said in an even toned voice that forced the listener to focus on the power of her words. "You're a very attractive young man with a tongue as slick as palm oil. I don't believe a word that flows from you. A man such as yourself would never be with a girl like her." She cast Tanna a brief look. "And do you want to know why?" she asked leaving no room for a reply. "Because you're a man who has a type. And your type is tall and slender and light brown, with a stylish taste in clothes. You may also wonder how I know this. It's because when I was checking into this facility, I saw you with a woman who fits that exact description." She looked at Tanna. "I know what you're up to." She shifted her gaze to him. "But not you. And that worries me. However, what will ease my worry is your promise that after this evening is through, we will never set eyes on you again. Is that clear?"

"Aunty," Tanna said, embarrassed for both of them. Logan was only trying to help her he didn't deserve a lecture. "It's just for one night, please let it pass and don't be so hard on him."

Her aunt maintained her stance, effectively blocking them. "He hasn't agreed yet."

"He will. He wants to, don't you?" When Logan didn't readily reply, his unreadable gaze fixed on Aunt Violet's face, Tanna filled in. "We met by accident, what are the chances we'll ever meet again. Please Aunty, let me have this moment, Mum looks so happy."

"Very well. One night, then you never do something like this again."

Tanna hugged her. "Thank you." She kissed her cheek. "I love you."

Her aunt brushed her away. "Foolish girl," but her words held a note of affection. She sent them one last look then walked away. Tanna watched several guests rush over to her.

"You don't know what you're in for," she said to Logan. "But thank you."

He shrugged. "Pretending to be a woman's boyfriend for the evening? How hard can it be?"

For him, clearly easy. He was a master. A master of charm and deception. Tanna wasn't sure if she should be impressed or nervous. She decided to be neither and just enjoy the rest of the evening. Within minutes he had her father's approval, her mother's devotion and her two sisters in awe.

"I guess we'll be hearing wedding bells soon," her mother said.

"Absolutely not," her father said. He was a man who matched his wife in height and breadth with a dark mustache and graying eyebrows. "You'll have to wait another two years, if you want anything like this." He made a broad gesture to indicate the cost of the wedding and elaborate reception, noting the opulence that surrounded them.

"Don't worry," Tanna said with a laugh. "We're taking things slow."

She broke free from her parents and mingled with other guests who were also eager to meet Tanna's mysterious boyfriend.

A woman, Tanna knew by sight but not by name, approached them. She was a well endowed woman both in the front and the back and wore a dress that proudly emphasized both. Her hair fell in rust colored blonde curls to her shoulders. She squinted her eyes and pointed at Logan. "I know I've seen you before and I never forget a face." She tapped her chin then wagged her finger. "Aren't you—?"

"No," he quickly said, interrupting her with a smile. "But I get that a lot."

"I could have sworn you were him. He—"

"Would be a very lucky man if he had a chance to make your acquaintance. Excuse me," he said, then guided Tanna away.

"Who does she think you are?"

"I have no idea, but I have the kind of face that people think they know me."

"You have a very distinctive face actually."

"What? Do you think you know me from somewhere too?"

Tanna didn't get a chance to reply because more people approached them. At one moment they were separated and Tanna saw Logan talking to the blonde woman alone. She couldn't make out what they were discussing but the woman seemed entranced. Not that Tanna found that surprising, Logan had that effect on people. When he finally returned to her side, she asked him about the woman and he just shrugged and said, "I had something I wanted to ask her," then effectively changed the subject. She knew better than to press him on it. Everyone was allowed their secrets.

An evening she'd initially couldn't wait to end, ended sooner than she'd expected. The last several hours had disappeared like minutes. Under a moonlight sky, and the sweet scent of fresh grass, they walked to one of the courtyard cottages where her room was. She'd told Logan he didn't have to escort her, but he'd insisted and she didn't want to discourage him. She liked his company and wanted to stay in it as long as she could. She didn't know how many drinks he'd had, but he walked with a careful measured gait that made her aware he'd consumed more than enough if he had to focus on walking with such care, and the activity lengthened their journey from the castle to their final destination.

Once they reached her cottage, Tanna led him up the wooden stairs. Each cottage was made up of three guest bedrooms. Her room was the last one down a short corridor. Too short. She'd wished there had been a long hallway—like the ones in the castle—that would take lots of time to get walk down.

Tanna stopped in front of her door, took a deep breath, then turned to him. It was time to say goodbye. Did she shake his hand? Give him a kiss? "I can't believe the night is over," she said with a smile so wide her aunt would have been pleased. "I don't know how to thank you."

"You already did."

"Or repay you."

He shoved his hands in his pockets. "You already have."

"I just got you a drink."

He looked at something over her head. "I needed it."

She nodded, surprised he was making no move to leave. "Well, I guess this is where we say goodbye," she said.

"Yes." He shifted his gaze to the floor and bit his lip. "Do you believe in fate?"

"Not really."

"Me neither," he said, keeping his gaze lowered, as well as his voice. "So I don't think we'll ever see each other again."

"Nope."

He lifted his gaze and his eyes clung to hers. "That's what I'm counting on." He swung her into the circle of his arms and covered her mouth with his. He didn't give her a moment to be surprised, pleasure followed too quickly making her forget everything else. Making her forget that she didn't really know him, that she'd never done something like this before.

His kiss sang through her veins, his mouth demanding a surrender she was too eager to give. That shocked her. His persuasive power over her. A man like him, one who could charm and lie so easily could be dangerous and she didn't want to be one of his prey.

She pushed him away. "You're drunk," she said breathless.

"I know."

"But I'm not and I'd be taking advantage of you."

He held out his arms. "I don't care."

"You will when you wake up tomorrow."

"That's if I remember anything."

"That's true," Tanna said, suddenly thoughtful. "You probably won't remember any of this"

"Probably."

"And we'll never meet again."

"Probably."

"So I—"

He promptly kissed away her response.

She let him, wrapping her arms around his neck.

And they kissed as if they didn't want to say goodbye, as if they wished they could make the night last forever.

Tanna was the first to pull away. "You'll get over her," she said, her lips burning, her heart racing, but her mind telling her that none of this was real.

"I don't want to talk about her right now." He drew her close again and trailed a series of kisses down the column of her neck, she could feel the heat of his hand on her back through her velvet bodice.

Tanna closed her eyes, indulging in the warm, wet feel of his mouth that touched and sucked her skin in varying intervals. "We have to stop now." She wasn't drunk, but he made her feel intoxicated.

"No, we don't."

"I don't do rebound sex, I'm sorry."

He straightened to his full height and folded his arms, his eyes lit with amusement. "Pity sex?"

"No," she said, unable to help a grin, "but I may consider comfort foreplay, but you'd have to hire someone else for the finale."

He started to return her grin then his brow raised a fraction and he pulled her close and spun her around. She didn't know the reason until she felt him wince and heard her aunt's voice. "Filthy talk again!"

Logan had shielded her from one of her aunt's blows, which he'd received instead. Tanna felt devastated and humiliated. Why did she have to come at the worst time? "Aunty!"

Aunt Violet moved to try to have another whack at Tanna, but he blocked her again.

"Aunty I was just—"

"I don't care." She grabbed for Tanna's wrist, but when Logan blocked her a third time, she glared at him. "You've done your job, now go," she said with a quick flip of her wrist.

"We're still saying goodbye," he said.

Her aunt narrowed her eyes. "In a few minutes you weren't planning to say anything." She rested a fist on her hip. "Goodbye Mr. Gibbs."

He looked at Tanna, who he still had safe in his embrace. "She's going to hit you real hard when I let you go, isn't she?"

"I'm used to it. It's a cultural thing."

He pressed a kiss on her forehead. "Bye, Tanna. It's been fun."

"Bye, Logan. I'll never—"

Aunt Violet clapped her hands together. "Are you filming a Nollywood drama? You've said your 'goodbyes' now go!"

He released Tanna then turned to Aunt Violet with a cold smile. "Saying goodbye to you is a pleasure," he said, then walked down the hall and disappeared down the stairs.

"I'm ashamed of you," Aunt Violet said, shoving Tanna inside her room.

Tanna stumbled in then caught herself on the armoire. "I was just—"

Aunt Violet raised her hand. "If you say 'trying to be funny' I'll hit you and I won't miss."

Tanna sat on her bed. "It doesn't matter now."

Aunt Violet stood by the door as if afraid Tanna would escape at any minute. "You sound disappointed."

"He saved me, Aunty. I had a wonderful time."

"He's a charming, dangerous man."

That was the best part. Who else would have pulled off a deception so smoothly? "I'm grateful to him all the same."

"You're smiling."

"I know."

"Do I need to lock you in your room?"

Tanna's smile fell. "I'm not that grateful."

"A few moments ago you looked pretty grateful to me," Aunt Violet said with a sniff.

Her face started to burn. How much had her aunt seen? "We were just saying goodbye."

"Those kind of goodbyes get women in trouble."

"Well, now he's out of my life so you have nothing to worry about." Tanna fluttered her lashes and wagged her finger at her aunt. "How could such a pretty woman wear such a sour expression?"

"You'll not contact this man again."

"I don't know anything else about him and I'm not interested to be honest. He's getting over a breakup and I don't fall for men on the rebound." She'd learned her lesson. The last two men she'd gotten on the rebound had ended up marrying other women. "I've never met him before and I know I'll never meet him again."

Her aunt pressed her finger against Tanna's mouth. "Shh…never tempt fate like that. You can never be sure of anything. Just say you don't think you will."

"Aunty. It's a big world with billions of people. What are the odds of us ever meeting again?"

Chapter Six

Two years later

There was nothing rosy or sweet about Rosemarie Lockley. She was a demanding, exacting, smart and impatient woman who liked to wear tailored suits in bright bold colors like purple and mauve. Today, neon green complemented her pecan colored skin, and heels like spikes exaggerated her height while diamond stud earrings glittered in her ears.

Tanna had taken the job on a referral, although she'd been warned by the estate agent that 'the bitch is an absolute nightmare'.

Tanna didn't see her that way. She saw a woman coming out of a divorce ready to move on with her life, but wanting to feel she was still in control. Tanna patiently answered Rosemarie's many questions, didn't feel offended when Rosemarie questioned her decisions or nitpicked at her suggestions. She didn't know the logistics of the divorce, but knew it was bitter and it was affecting Rosemarie hard. Tanna liked clients like Rosemarie, they kept her on her toes, they pushed her to be better and pleasing one of them was more gratifying than the ones who gushed at everything she did. Rosemarie wouldn't gush. She barely even offered faint praise, gaining her approval would be monumental.

But professional prestige and success wasn't the only reason she'd been grateful for the job with Rosemarie. Difficult clients like Rosemarie came with a healthy profit. The money she'd make would help her surprise her friend, Ambrosia. Ambrosia's daughter was facing a series of medical tests, to diagnosis an illness that continued to baffle her doctors, and her friend couldn't afford to cover them all. The money Tanna would be able to give her, would put her halfway there. She just needed another four thousand to reach her goal of getting the tests fully paid for.

Tanna waited in the family room while Rosemarie did her inspection of the changes, not that much needed to be done. Any identifying photos of the couple had already been stored—thrown?—away. The Dutch colonial, tucked away in an expensive Washington DC suburb, was lovely, with only a few personal distinctions such as Rosemarie's Japanese mask collection which had to also be put in storage. Tanna had improved on the landscaping to give the house added curb appeal. She hadn't had to deal with outdated furniture or old appliances. Her main job had been moving pictures and re-painting some rooms. Rosemarie had one large painting of a dark, disturbing landscape, over a couch. When Tanna had offered to move it out of view, underneath it she'd found a hole in the wall—the size of a fist.

"My ex liked to throw tantrums," Rosemarie said, as if on the verge of a yawn. "You'll see more of his little tantrums that will need to be cleaned up.

Tanna found more than a few. There had been a large wine stain in the upstairs bedroom and another hole that appeared to have been made by a foot. It was a gorgeous house filled with horrible secrets. What kind of man had she put up with? Tanna knew she'd never know and truthfully, wondered how such a sophisticated woman could have fallen for such a man, but knew it wasn't her place to ask.

"He only touched the walls," Rosemarie said one day as she finished a glass of red wine while Tanna inspected another hole hidden by the hanging pots in the kitchen. She hadn't asked, but she had been curious. Over the several days she worked on staging the home, Rosemarie absently shared some of her tales. Most times, Tanna didn't know what to say, so she pretended not to hear her. Today, however, there would be no more revelations. Everything was in place. The house was ready for buyers, but first it had to pass Rosemarie's inspection.

Minutes later Rosemarie appeared in the entryway wearing a frown. Not that it mattered much. She was still stunning with smooth skin, a pert nose, high cheekbones and the nonchalant beauty of the wealthy. She didn't look as if she'd reached forty yet, but moved with the tired, burdened movements of someone much older.

Tanna pulled out her pen, ready to take notes. Rosemarie usually frowned like that when she had a complaint. Had she changed her mind about the neutral tones in the sitting room? Did she want less lighting in the hallway?

"You've done a magnificent job."

Tanna blinked, not sure she'd heard correctly. Had Rosemarie actually praised her? She'd said the words so quickly and in such a dry, disinterested tone, she wasn't sure. "I'm sorry?"

"I said you've done a magnificent job."

Not good, not great, but magnificent. Was she feeling okay? "Thank you."

Rosemarie sat down and crossed her legs. "Everything they say about you is true. You do work wonders. If I didn't live here, I'd buy the house myself. You made it feel like a home."

"I'm glad you're pleased."

"I'm more than pleased. You're a miracle worker."

Tanna felt a little light headed. Rosemarie was pleased? Happy? It was hard to take because the other woman's expression didn't change, her mouth still curved down at the corner, her tone still held a note of ennui but her words…her words were like firecrackers bursting in beauty among a dark sky. She'd succeeded!

"Thank you."

Rosemarie turned towards the window when she heard a car drive up. "That will be my brother. I wanted him to see the changes you made."

Tanna put her pen and notebook in her handbag. "Then I will leave you two. Good luck on the house sale."

Rosemarie sighed and shook her head. "I never need luck when it comes to business, it's men where my luck falls short."

Tanna cleared her throat feeling uncomfortable, again not knowing what to say. "Then best of luck in the future." She gathered her handbag as she heard the front door open then close.

"I'm impressed, Sis," came a deep male voice from the foyer. "I see what you mean. The landscape looks great."

"Doran, we're in the living room," she called out to him.

The owner of the voice then appeared in the entryway and froze.

Tanna saw him and jumped to her feet as if propelled by springs. It couldn't be him. Him! But it was. And suddenly two years felt like minutes. Minutes ago they were in a castle, the moonlight whispering along the corridor while he held her in his arms and kissed her as if he'd never let her go. As if there would be no tomorrow.

"Oh my God!" She didn't mean to speak. The words escaped before she could hold them back.

He stared at her, his expression enigmatic. She knew he recognized her, but she doubted he remembered their kiss. His gaze was too distant and calculating to hint at any brief remembrance of passion, making it clear that only she felt the burden of a flood of emotions—desire, disbelief, regret. Not much had changed about him except that he wasn't bald anymore, although he kept his dark hair short, and had a mustache.

How could this be? What were the chances? And did Rosemarie call him Doran not Logan?

"You two know each other?" Rosemarie said. "I ask that knowing that you do," she said, offering her brother a smile that was as cuddly as a crocodile, "so don't try to lie to me."

"Yes," Tanna said when Doran remained mute. "We met..." She stopped when she saw him tense his brows and give a brief shake of his head. "...at another house showing."

Rosemarie turned to her brother surprised. "You didn't tell me you were looking for another property."

"Just browsing," he said.

"Like you do everything. No sense of commitment. And why didn't you tell me about her? Planning to keep her all to yourself?"

He leaned against the doorframe. "I got busy."

"That's my brother trying to be funny," she said to Tanna. "He's never busy."

Tanna gripped the strap of her handbag. "I should go."

"And he's never serious about anything," Rosemarie continued. "He's not serious about the family business, he breezes through women and changes residences like they're shoes. If you could change men as well as you do houses, I'd hire you again."

Tanna cleared her throat, wary. "Yes, well—"

"It's better to change than to stay with something too long," Doran said.

"I wanted my marriage to work."

"You mean you wanted your image to last."

Rosemarie's lips tightened. "I did what I had to do."

"You mean you stayed in hell so that you could keep the devil off your back."

Tanna shifted sideways towards the door hoping they wouldn't notice.

Rosemarie shrugged without care. "I did my part, you're in Mom's sights now."

"She won't get me in her clutches."

Rosemarie's crocodile grin returned. "She already has a woman in mind."

"Who?"

"I wasn't going to tell you this because it was supposed to be a surprise, but I just can't wait to see the look on your face."

Tanna shifted another few inches as Doran's gaze sharpened.

"What?" he said.

"Megan has been asking about you. She's single again and Mom's determined to get you two back together. So don't be too surprised when she makes an appearance at the lake house for Mom's summer party."

Tanna halted. *Megan?* The same Megan who'd broken his heart and run off with her father's lawyer? *That* Megan wanted him back? Tanna stole a glance at his face, sensed his iron-clad control, but his expression gave nothing away.

"She's too late," he said. "I already have a woman."

"You always have a woman," Rosemarie said with a sniff, unimpressed. "Do you think that will make a difference?"

"Yes, because this woman is my fiancée."

Rosemarie shook her head. "That's a likely story."

"It's true."

She patted the empty space beside her. "Come and sit down so you can lie to me in comfort. You know I don't bite."

He didn't move.

Rosemarie uncrossed her legs and leaned forward in amazement. "You're actually considering marrying one of those long-legged numbskulls you like showing off at parties?"

"No. She's not like that. She's not my usual type."

"Have I met her?"

"Yes."

"Who is she?" Rosemarie asked for the first time not sounding bored or disinterested. "What does she do?"

Doran nodded at Tanna who now stood only two feet away from him. "She works miracles."

Chapter Seven

*O*h *no. This was not good.* Tanna felt Rosemarie's keen, razor sharp gaze, beads of sweat forming on her forehead. What was he doing? No, she knew what he was doing. But *why* was he doing it? No, she knew the answer to that too, but it still didn't make her feel better. She felt trapped. Unlike at her sisters' wedding where she knew the role to play, here she felt unsure. He was a master deceiver, but she wasn't so sure she could do the same. Especially with a woman like Rosemarie

"I was going to tell you," he added. "But was waiting for the right moment."

Rosemarie glanced at Tanna's hand. "Where's the ring?"

"I haven't bought it yet."

"How long have you known each other?"

"Six months."

"You're lying."

Doran nodded. "You're right. We're not engaged yet. The truth is, Tanna didn't know about this moment. She didn't know that I was going to ask her to share her life with me. We've been seeing each other quietly and that's all I can say."

Tanna stared at him dumbfounded. How could he lie so convincingly? He'd fooled her family, but could he fool his sister?

Rosemarie was silent for a long moment then said, "I don't believe you. You expect me to believe that you're with her?" She turned to Tanna. "No offense, but you're just too smart for someone like him and he's just the kind of person to play a trick like this."

"It's not a trick. I'm serious."

"He likes his women the dumber the better," she continued as if he hadn't spoken, "so that he doesn't have to work that hard to impress them. He's all flash and no substance."

"Tanna knows me better than you do."

"Is that right?" She studied Tanna's face. "Then tell me something I don't know."

Tanna froze, her gaze darting between them. He'd put her on the spot. Why had he put her on the spot? What did he expect her to say? "Well…umm…I'm sure you know as much as I do."

"Such as?"

"The fact that he's really smart—"

"Doran? Smart?" Rosemarie threw her head back and laughed.

Tanna cringed wondering where she'd went wrong. She wasn't trying to be funny. She looked at Doran who had his hands in his pockets, his jaw tense.

"Street smart," he said. "That's what she meant."

Tanna shook her head, "No, I meant—" But his sharp gaze stopped her from finishing. She didn't know why he didn't want his sister to think he was smart. "Yes, that's right. Street smart."

"Which street?" Rosemarie asked, wiping away tears. "Wisconsin Avenue? Park Avenue? Rodeo Drive?" She laughed harder.

Tanna glanced at Doran again expecting to see him upset, instead he looked bored and when he caught her staring, he winked.

Rosemarie patted the couch again. "Why won't you two sit down?"

Tanna sent a desperate look at Doran then past him at the front door out of reach. "I really have to go."

Rosemarie sat back and crossed her legs again. "Before you give him your answer?" she asked, her tone sounding bored again, but this time it held a touch of cruel amusement.

"My answer?"

"Yes, my brother just admitted that his proposal is spur of the moment and caught you by surprise. So will you marry him or not?"

Tanna swallowed then licked her lips. "Well…yes. Of course."

"You don't sound sure."

"It's a little overwhelming."

"I bet it is," Rosemarie said with a knowing look. She leaned back in her seat. "Don't let me stop you."

"From what?"

"When my ex asked me to marry him, I fell into his arms. I realize that was a mistake now, but I still did it because I was so happy."

"Tanna's shy," Doran said. "She doesn't show affection in front of an audience."

"Very well," Rosemarie said with a shrug. "Mom is going to have a coronary when she meets her." She rubbed her hands together as if gleefully anticipating something awful. "Tell me she's first generation at least."

"Came here when she was seven."

"Salt into the wound."

"Is that a problem?" Tanna asked.

"Mom's a little testy when it come to immigrants," Rosemarie said. "Not that I care, dear, I'm sure my brother sees it as part of your charm."

Tanna looked at Doran with pleading eyes. There was just enough room to squeeze past him, but doing so would look undignified. "I really should go."

He moved out of the way. "I'll walk you to your car."

"Goodbye," Tanna said.

"No," Rosemarie replied with a wave of her hand. "Until we meet again."

⋈

"You don't have to follow me to my car," Tanna said as he walked her down the driveway to her Honda Civic the summer sun making the grey finish look white. She heard bees buzzing nearby as they busied themselves pollinating the roses that lined the pathway.

"Yes, I do." He motioned to his black Porsche. "I parked behind you."

Tanna unlocked her car with a push of her key, using more force than necessary. *He was going to move his car.* And here she'd thought he'd wanted her alone for another reason. She should have known better. What had she expected him to do? Reminisce over old times? They hadn't even known each other a day. Just one wonderful night and he'd forgotten the best part of it.

She heard him make a muffled sound and turned to him. She saw an expression of cynical amusement on his face.

"What is it?" she asked.

"Fate has a sense of humor."

Tanna threw up her hands exasperated. "I know! Isn't this crazy? It's impossible."

Doran shook his head. "Improbable, not impossible."

She pointed at him. "See? You are smart. Why did you want me to pretend that you're not?"

He rubbed the back of his neck. "I'm not that smart."

Tanna folded her arms.

"It's a long story." He headed for his car then spun around and walked back to her. "I don't know why you turn up when I need you most, but I'm going to seize this opportunity and not ask questions. I need your help."

Tanna paused. "More than pretending to be your fiancée in front of your sister?" She gestured to the house. "I may have lost a great client referral because of this. What if she finds out I lied to her?"

"She won't and if she does, I'll make it up to you. But I just need you to do one more thing."

"What?" Tanna held up her hand. "And please don't tell me you want me to meet your mother."

Doran looked at her, the expression is his eyes not exactly a plea, but close.

Tanna shook her head. "No, *Logan*," she said using the false name he'd given at the castle.

"I used that name to get into character." He took a step closer and lowered his voice. "I just need you for a few days," he said before she could speak. He closed her car door. "We'll go to my family's lake house and you'll pretend to be my fiancée."

Before she could respond, he bent down and kissed her on the cheek.

Tanna gaped at him startled, cupping her cheek like a love struck teenager, her skin tingling where his lips had touched her. "What was that?"

"My sister's watching," he said, turning her so that her back was to the window. "Anybody ever tell you that you have a very animated face?"

"No."

"That's why I have to have you facing me otherwise it will give us away."

"Then maybe you should have chosen someone else to pretend to be your fiancée."

"No, you're perfect." He removed something from her hair, his fingers brushing her cheek.

She pushed his hand away. "Cut that out."

"There really was something in your hair," Doran said, showing her a piece of fuzz before he released it. He pulled out his cell phone, then held his hand out for hers. "I'll let you go and then call you with the plan."

She absently handed him her cell phone. "Do you know how hard it was for me to convince your sister? And in case it escaped your notice, she wasn't entirely convinced. Is your mother any better?"

He exchanged contact information on their phones then handed hers back to her. "No, she's worse."

"Worse?"

"Yes," he said with a nod, tucking his phone away.

Tanna blinked several times, not knowing what to think. "And you want me to get her to accept me as her possible daughter-in-law?"

"No. I don't want her to like you."

"What?"

He pulled her close and kissed her, this time on the mouth. "I'll explain everything later, darling," he said with a wink then raced to his car jumped inside before she could ask him not to kiss her like that.

It wasn't real, but she enjoyed it way too much.

"I don't believe you," Rosemarie said the moment Doran stepped back inside the house.

"You don't believe what?" he asked, collapsing into the loveseat in front of her.

"I don't believe you're really seeing that woman." She tapped her chest. "If I can't believe it you can't get Mom to believe it either. So whatever scheme you're up to, you'd better come up with something else."

"It's not a scheme. How I feel about Tanna took me by surprise too."

"So you're really going to introduce her to Mom?"

"Yes."

Rosemarie frowned then said, "Are you doing this because of Mom or because of Megan? You never told me what happened between you two."

Doran shrugged. "We broke up. There's nothing more to say."

"Then why won't you show up at the lake house alone and be there for her? I'm sure she'd love to have someone's wide shoulders to cry on. Are you still certain it shouldn't be yours?"

"I'm with Tanna now."

"So you're completely over her?" Doran sent her such a dark look, Rosemarie raised her hands in surrender. "Okay, okay. I believe it's over."

But even as she said the words Doran knew it was a lie. He wasn't over Megan. Two years later and his heart still raced at the sound of her name, he still remembered the taste of her lips, the feel of her body. For years he'd dreamed of winning her back. Of showing her that he was more of a man than Adam. That she'd made a mistake by cheating on him, but now he didn't want her back. He wanted to make her realize what she had lost.

Chapter Eight

He could convince an Eskimo to buy snow.

Tanna dusted the wooden carvings—one of a woman carrying a water jug on her head, and another holding a fruit—on her bookshelf while listening to Doran, surprised that his plan actually made sense. He wanted her to annoy his mother so that when they broke up, his mother would be so relieved that they weren't getting married she'd leave him alone for years to come. As crazy as it sounded, the plan had its own strange logic. And she could understand why he'd asked her. A woman who hired an escort to her sisters' wedding wasn't above a little deception, but she didn't want to sound too compliant. He only wanted her for several days, but every plan needed to have certain details ironed out and she knew she had to be cautious. She closed the blinds to her apartment, the night sky black with the arrival of the evening.

"I understand your reasoning," she said once he'd finished speaking, "but your plan seems a little cruel. I'm sure she just wants to see you happy." She dusted a side table.

"When you meet her, you won't feel that way. You'll earn every cent."

She paused midway with the duster in her hand. "Earn?"

"Didn't I mention payment?"

"No."

"Five thousand."

"Five thousand dollars?"

"Were you thinking pounds?" he asked with a smile in his voice.

She wasn't in the mood for teasing. She had to make sure she was hearing correctly. Money like that would be a dream come true. She'd have enough to help Ambrosia. Tanna slowly sat on her couch not sure her legs could hold her. "You'd pay me five thousand dollars to pretend to be your girlfriend?"

"Fiancée," he corrected.

"You'd pay me that much to be your fiancée?"

"Yes."

The duster fell from her hand. "I don't believe this."

"Why? Is it too little or too much?"

It was just right! He'd shown up just when she needed him too. Perhaps fate wasn't so awful after all. "Okay, I'll do it. What exactly do you want me to do?"

"Annoy her."

"You have to be a little more specific than that. What gets on her nerves? What kind of girlfriends didn't she like?"

He fell silent.

"What's wrong?"

"I don't want to make you mad."

"Why would you make me mad?"

"I chose you for a reason. You're exactly the kind of woman who would annoy her, so just showing up will be enough."

"What's wrong with me?" Tanna said outraged.

"I didn't say anything is wrong with you."

She picked up the duster and absently hit the front of the couch with it. "Then why wouldn't she like me?"

"Tanna, I really don't think you want to know."

"Yes, I do."

Doran sighed. "Well, she likes women who are fit."

She set the duster down beside her. "I'm not fat."

"I didn't say you were. But I can guess you don't run five miles a day or even know what a gym membership looks like."

"You didn't need to add the second part and I'll have you know that I'm very healthy."

"See? I told you you'd get mad."

"I'm not mad," she said, trying not to shout. "Go on."

"Are you a glutton for punishment?"

"Yes, now go on."

"You weren't born here."

Tanna nodded. That didn't bother her as much, she was used to it. "Do you want me to put on an accent? I can do the ignorant immigrant, the naïve non-native or the amorous African."

"The what?"

68   Dara Girard

"Oh sah!" she mimicked in a high voice. "I am so happy to be in dis country! Praise de Lawd Almighty!"

Doran cleared his throat. "No, you won't need to go that far."

"Are you sure?"

"Yes, I don't think it will work if I start laughing."

"Really?" she said pleased that he found her funny. "If you thought that was good let me do my impression of my grandmother when she's bartering at the market."

"Wait until we're there, I'm sure my mother would love it."

"You're being sarcastic."

"Completely."

"Fine," Tanna said resigned. "I'll do my best to be myself and irritate her."

"Good. But I need you to understand one thing," he said, his tone growing serious. "I'm going to make this relationship as real as possible, which mean I'm going to be…hands on."

Tanna didn't misunderstand. "Your hands are allowed around my waist and in my hand, that's all."

"Nope, you have to add your face, neck, back, arms, legs and feet."

Tanna felt her face burn at the thought of his hands traveling there. "That's a lot of places."

"Consider the places I didn't mention."

I don't want to. But her mind went there anyway. She pictured them alone in the cottage, him kissing her senseless, his hands unlatching her bra, sneaking down her panties. She squeezed her eyes shut and imagined Aunt Violence giving her a hard whack on the head saying, 'You bad girl!' "Why would you need to touch my legs and feet?"

"I'll find a reason. Do you agree?"

She sighed. He was probably just trying to annoy her, nothing would happen. "Sure."

"Okay, how about my mouth?"

She paused unsure she'd heard correctly. "Your what?"

"My mouth. Since you want to be specific, where can my mouth go?"

His mouth? Why was he talking about his mouth? The same mouth she remembered leaving sucking kisses on her neck. She could imagine his mouth on her shoulders, slowly trailing down her chest…"You can kiss me freely on the lips."

"Just the lips? No, that won't work. Add hands, face, neck and shoulders then we have a deal."

"No shoulders," she said quickly, her mind repeating her naughty fantasy.

"Why not?"

"There's no reason for you to kiss my shoulders," she said, knowing her resistance sounded lame. "I never wear anything strapless so it would look silly anyway."

"Fine. How often?"

Tanna shifted in her seat, wishing she didn't suddenly feel so warm. "How often for what?"

"How often can I kiss you?"

Would this conversation never end? "Once a day."

"Cute. For what I'm paying, you're lucky I'm even asking. I want seven times."

"Who needs to kiss seven times a day?" her voice cracked.

"I like to keep my options open."

"Four."

"Five. I want my mother to really think we're in love."

She sighed in defeat. "Fine, five and I'll be counting."

"And I'll chose when and how. Don't worry, I won't embarrass you with too much affection."

"Of course."

"But don't get confused, okay? I don't want you falling for me."

"Relax, you're not my type."

"Yes, most ladies say that before I change their minds," he said, then disconnected.

Tanna glared at the phone. She considered calling him back with a witty retort, unfortunately none came to mind. She'd just show him that she wouldn't fall for him. True, she found him attractive—beautifully, devastating, wonderfully attractive—but she'd seen his face when Rosemarie had mentioned Megan. His expression hadn't changed, but she saw a flash of longing and hurt in his dark gaze, maybe even a tensing of his jaw but she wasn't sure.

She held up her phone as if he were still on the line, glad she'd finally come up with a good retort. "Don't worry, I'm too smart to fall for a man who's still in love with another woman."

Chapter Nine

"You don't find this the least bit insulting?" her best friend, Ambrosia Raven, said. They sat poolside in two lounge chairs under an umbrella at the local swim club, while they chaperoned Ambrosia's eight year old daughter, Hallie, and her four cousins ranging in age from ten to fifteen. "Hey, I said no splashing," she said to one of them, her voice carrying further than a lifeguard with a megaphone among the sound of children's high pitched squeals and adults' chatter. She turned back to Tanna, and pointed to herself. "I do." She glanced at her watch. "Do you think I should put more sunscreen on them?"

Tanna looked at the large tube peeking out of her friend's bag. "It's not even been an hour yet. Besides, they still look like zebras," she said, noting the stripes of white residue that hadn't blended into their skin yet. Her friend tended to worry; she'd been that way since college when she got a B minus in a computer course and feared her Egyptian-American father and Canadian mother would disown her. She kept her coal black hair shoulder length and had classically attractive features, which dew enough male attention when she wasn't shouting like a soccer mom on the sidelines.

Ambrosia nodded. "You're right and so am I."

"About what?"

"The fact that this guy is insulting you."

"What's insulting about five thousand dollars?"

"Forget about the money and think about the reason. He's chosen you specifically because he knows his mother won't like you."

"I really don't care."

"You should care. I know you don't need the money." She turned to the pool. "What did I tell you about splashing? And no dunking," she said her command immediately getting results.

"No, I don't need the money," Tanna said, pulling out a check from her purse. She handed it to Ambrosia. "But you do."

Her friend stared at it, making no move to touch it. "What is this?"

"I know Hallie needs more tests and your deductible hasn't been met yet."

Ambrosia's eyes filled with tears. "Tanna, don't do this."

"I'm her godmother, right? Of course I want her to have the best." The software company where her friend worked had been bought and she'd been downsized to a position that didn't pay as well as her previous one, although she was glad to still have a job. Her husband worked out-of- state for a construction company that didn't get as many jobs as it needed to. He came home on the weekend, but many times her friend felt like a single parent. Being in the pool was one of the few things Hallie could still enjoy. She was thin for her age due to her picky eating habits, had tender joints and some days could hardly rise from her bed or the couch due to exhaustion.

Ambrosia covered her face. "You don't know how much this will help us."

"Yes, I do," Tanna said, pleased to hear the joy in her friend's voice. "Why do you think I took Rosemarie Lockley on as a client? And with his money your financial concerns are over."

Ambrosia shook her head. "But you can't do this for me. I won't let you."

"It's just for a few days. Make the appointments and stop worrying about me."

She hugged her. "You're the best."

"I try."

"But this still won't work," Ambrosia said with a frown. "Your parents haven't let you forget your last break up."

"There's no reason for them to know anything about this."

Ambrosia stared down at the check for a long moment then held it out to Tanna. "As much as I need this, I can't let you be used like this."

Tanna pushed her hand away. "I'm not being used." She nodded to the check. "Now put it away, before the wind blows it into the pool."

There was no wind, but Ambrosia got the hint and promptly did as told. "So what's wrong with him?"

"Why should there be anything wrong with him?"

She set her bag back down. "He's asking you to pretend to be his girlfriend, don't you find that weird? I mean, only desperate people hire others too..." Her words trailed away when Tanna sent her a significant look. "Your situation was different. People fake things at weddings all the time."

"I had an invisible boyfriend for three months, pretended a stranger was him for a night and then broke up with him after the wedding."

"Okay, maybe you both are crazy." She abruptly surged to her feet and pointed to one of the children. "If I have to warn you again, I'm sucking you out of the water like a straw. Is that clear?" She waited a moment—making sure her glare said all that it needed—then sat back down. "What were we talking about?"

"Crazy behavior," Tanna said.

Ambrosia tucked a strand of hair behind her ear. "Yes, that's right."

"You just don't know what it's like to have people trying to match you up every minute of the day as if your singleness was a curable disease."

"True, but I still find his reason insulting. You're pretty, smart and successful. Why wouldn't his mother like you?"

Tanna raised her shoulders, feigning nonchalance. "There are reasons," she said, not wanting to tell her friend what they were. "But I don't care. He's not my type."

"I looked him up. I've seen his picture."

Tanna smiled with a look of triumph. "But have you seen the picture of the woman he's in love with?" she asked knowing that she hadn't.

Her friend's eyes widened. "Is this woman also someone his mother doesn't approve of?" She clasped her hands together. "I get it now, it's the lesser of two evils. If his mother won't agree to his first choice she'll have to accept his second."

"Something like that," Tanna said, although she knew that wasn't his strategy at all. "Trust me. At the end of this, you'll be getting the remaining balance, Doran will get his mother off his back and we'll all be happy."

"I don't know what you're getting out of this."

Tanna squeezed her arm. "Helping you is all that matters to me." Her cell phone rang. She checked the number. "It's him."

"Maybe he's changed his mind. Maybe he's calling to cancel." Ambrosia grabbed her bag, put it on her lap and dug for her purse. "Maybe he wants his money back."

Tanna snatched the bag from her then set it heavily on the ground afraid it would tip her chair over. "I doubt it," she said before answering. "Hello, the amazingly attractive and elegant Tanna speaking. How may I help you?"

"There's been a change of plans."

Her shoulders dropped. There was no smile in his voice. He was going to cancel as Ambrosia had feared. She could feel her friend's anxious gaze on her. She'd have to come up with the money another way. "Hold on a minute," she said to him, stood then walked outside the pool gates for privacy. "You're getting back with Megan?"

"No, I—"

"Your mother left the country?"

Doran sighed in frustration. "What have I told you—"

"About not interrupting. I know, I'm sorry. Damn, I just did it again, didn't I? I don't usually I just…and now I'm rambling so I'll stop and let you speak."

"Thank you. The thing is—"

"I really didn't mean to cut you off like that and jump to conclusions. That was unfair….hello? Hello? Are you still there?"

"Only if you're finished."

"Yes. Go on….I'm waiting," she said when he didn't speak.

"I'm just making sure."

"Ziiiippp!"

"What was that?" he asked.

"That's the sound of me zipping my lips."

"Okay," he said, but she couldn't tell if he was amused or annoyed.

She didn't want to annoy him. She wanted to continue with his plan. She switched the phone to her other ear and took a deep breath. No matter what he said she could handle it.

"I called because there's been a change of plans and if you interrupt me by saying 'What?' I'm hanging up."

She made a cry of protest.

"What did you say?"

Tanna made a motion of unzipping her lips even though he couldn't see her. "I said I wasn't going to say anything."

"Good. You're self-employed, right?"

"Yes, I run my own business. Why?"

"Before you meet my mother, I need to show you off."

"Show me off?"

"Yes, for about two weeks so clear your schedule and be ready tonight."

"I thought the five thousand dollars was just for the weekend?"

"I mentioned several days, remember?"

He had. She knew she should have been more specific. "Yes, but—"

"See you tonight." He disconnected.

Tanna stared at the phone wishing he didn't have a habit of doing that. She returned to her friend and sat down.

"What did he say?" Ambrosia asked, her eyes wide.

"He wants my schedule to be free for the next two weeks so that he can 'show me off'."

"What does that mean?"

Tanna shrugged. "I have no idea."

Chapter Ten

Tanna found out soon enough when Doran whisked her off to a celebrity wedding in Morocco. Took her dancing at a nightclub in Monte Carlo, wined and dined her in a villa in Turks and Caicos then escorted her to the private island party of an eccentric billionaire Doran affectionately called "The Loon".

She was never without the finest clothes to wear or the most sparkling of jewelry. In public, Doran held her close, whispered silly jokes in her ear, introduced her as if she were a treasure he'd discovered. But in private he was a different man. A man she couldn't quite read. He talked without revealing much about himself. She wondered if she could loosen his tongue with alcohol as she had on their first meeting, but every attempt ended in failure.

Tanna looked at him as they flew back from a brief trip to Barbados on his private jet. It had plush light grey lounge chairs and luxurious cabin space. Doran lay stretched out on the couch, watching an action film on the TV, looking very much like the carefree playboy his sister had described. Tanna studied his handsome profile not sure she really liked him, not that it mattered, that wasn't her job. But she wondered if it had only been the liquor and desperation that had made her see him in a different light when they were at the castle.

Even in the weeks they'd been together, his passing kisses hadn't aroused her as that first kiss had. But his present kisses had been very superficial—a light peck on the cheek here, a brief brush of the lips there. She felt a little disappointed because she didn't want to see this side of him. It had been more enjoyable thinking of him as the fantasy hero she'd met at her sisters' wedding. But that hero was definitely gone. In two years a hard edge had developed around him. She knew she was in no danger of falling for a man like him whose heart most definitely belonged to someone else.

"I think you've made your point," she said, as he watched a shootout scene he'd seen three times before. It was a bloody, gory film that appeared to be his favorite. He even smiled at the same places. "I had fun, although I think you went a little overboard."

"How?" he asked, lifting the sparkling glass of water the steward had set down for him.

She waited for the sight of a car exploding, a part of the film that always made him laugh, filling the cabin with the sound of shattering glass, metal being blown apart and scorching flames, then said, "Who attends this many functions in two weeks?"

"I do." He took a long swallow then set the glass down. "The only difference this time is that I'm with the same woman more than once."

"And that hasn't happened since…" She stopped, leaving the question in the air.

He replayed the car explosion scene. "You've succeeded with the easy part. Now the real work begins." He turned to her and flashed a roguish grin before he glanced at her hand. "Dear."

She looked down at the engagement ring on her finger. The stone was so big it was almost an embarrassment. It was how she'd felt the first time she saw it, but he'd insisted she try it on, then she couldn't get it off so she feigned delight, forcing him to buy it. Another man may have taken umbrage on how much it had cost him, but Doran appeared unperturbed.

After she met his mother, she was going to fast until she lost enough weight to get the blasted ring off her finger and hand it back to him.

"It looks good on you."

She didn't know what to make of that statement so she looked at the film. "Now that's what I call a bonfire," she said saying the lines of the main hero.

Doran sat up and stared at her surprised. "You've seen this before?"

Tanna stared back at him. Was he serious? He'd seen the same film in the hotel in Morocco, again in the villa, another time on the flight back from Monte Carlo and now. She was with him each time, didn't he remember that? "Um…Yes."

"Isn't it great?" he said with more enthusiasm than he'd shown the entire time they'd been together.

"Yes."

His whole face spread into a smile. "What's your favorite part?"

Tanna chewed her lower lip as if thinking then said, "The car explosion."

He punched his fist into the palm of his other hand and the hard edges fell away from his features, making him look like a little boy who'd made a new friend. "Mine too! It just hits it, right?"

"With perfection," she said, feeling a little guilty for lying to him. But the happy expression on his face made the feeling fade. If a little lie could make him look like that, she'd lie all the way home. "Everything comes together at that moment."

"I know. Not everybody gets that."

She turned back to the film. "Oh, and this is another good part," she said pointing to the screen. "The ambush. When Taylor's betrayed by his friend. That's the worse. I never saw it coming."

"Me neither," Doran said in a low voice as he returned his gaze to the screen.

And they watched the climactic scene in silence, but to her surprise Tanna soon noticed Doran looking at her more than the film. When she glanced at him, he quickly looked away, but she felt a new awareness in the air, the sudden heightened awareness of a gazelle sensing a lion in the distance—anticipation, as she sensed him starting to look at her in a new, exciting way.

Don't fall for it, her mind told her. He didn't see her as a woman, he only saw her as a prop in his deception.

But with every glance he sent her way, there was a tingling in the pit of her stomach, the cabin suddenly felt too small, her body felt too hot.

Don't fall for him, her mind warned her, but she knew she was in danger of doing just that.

Chapter Eleven

aisy Garth loved her men with beards, her vodka straight up and her gossip hot. She jogged around the tree lined track of the Ola Day Spa. At fifty-nine she was determined to keep her figure for her latest boy toy—a souvenir from Antigua. But today she couldn't concentrate on the physical activity as her mind hummed with the latest news.

"I saw your son with a woman," she said to her companion, Vanessa Gibson, who easily kept pace with her. She jogged with the ease of someone born for the task, her brown skin untouched by the slightest hint of sweat.

"Which one?" Vanessa said. "The boring one or the naughty one?"

Daisy laughed harder than the comment warranted, but she was building up to the real topic and that always made her giddy. "Who else?"

"Doran is always with a woman."

"Not just any woman. He seemed serious about this one."

"He hasn't been serious in years."

"He's serious now."

Vanessa paused. "Why do you say that?"

"Ellen saw him in a jewelry store."

"That's also nothing new."

"She saw him buying rings."

Vanessa slowed her pace. "Rings?"

"To be more specific an engagement ring."

"You're sure you're not mistaken?"

"A woman was with him."

Vanessa halted and stared at her. "What!"

Daisy nodded at her friend's outraged expression. "Yes."

"That's impossible. How can I not know anything about it?"

"I'm sure you've heard enough about him. He's had tongues wagging from Morocco to Barbados."

Vanessa turned and started to jog again, although at a slower pace. "I'm always hearing things about him, I've learned not to listen. Who is this woman? What's her name? What is she like?"

"Do you really want to know?"

"No, I asked because I enjoy the sound of my voice. Of course I want to know."

"Then let me show you," Daisy said. She stopped and pulled out her cell phone. Once she found the image she was looking for she held the screen up for Vanessa to see.

Vanessa's face paled. "Oh no."

Daisy's grin increased, sharing this news was even better than she'd hoped. "Yes."

"But she looks very…"

"African?"

Vanessa nodded.

"I've heard that she *is*. At least she's pretty even if she's—"

Vanessa shook her head. "No. I won't allow it."

"It will be hard to stop him. He couldn't keep his hands off her."

"It's a phase that will pass."

"And if it doesn't?"

Vanessa's gaze grew cold. "That's not an option."

The call came sooner than expected, but it wasn't a surprise. Doran glanced at the number on his phone as he lay on his couch watching a TV sitcom. He'd planned for this moment, he'd chosen the place to buy Tanna's engagement ring with particular care. He knew it wouldn't take long for news to get back to his mother.

He picked up the phone. "Who told you?"

"I'm not in a good mood right now."

"I thought you'd be pleased. You wanted me to settle down, right?"

"Don't be facetious."

"Don't be what?" he asked feigning ignorance.

She sighed loudly, which was uncharacteristic of her. She usually kept her feelings to herself, but he knew how to push her buttons.

"How much did you spend?"

Daron clicked his tongue in a gentle scold. "Didn't you teach me that talking about money is crass?"

"She's a gold digger. It's as clear to me as anything. How can you think of marrying a woman who comes out of nowhere?"

"She didn't come out of nowhere."

"I wasn't going to tell you this, but Megan is free."

"You say that like I'm supposed to care."

"You two make an excellent couple. I don't know what happened—"

"No, you don't."

"But every worthwhile relationship hits a rough patch....Doran?" she said when he didn't reply.

"I'm still waiting for the part where I'm supposed to care."

"This is too important for you to be glib. Not only would it be a good match, but think of the connections."

"We don't need her connections. I think—"

"Oh dear, when have you started doing that? Haven't you noticed that you aren't good at it?"

Doran gritted his teeth. "I still think—"

"Megan will be at the summer party. I expect you to be your usual charming self. Give her a chance. When she spoke to me the other day, she made it clear how unhappy she is that things didn't work out."

She was only unhappy that things hadn't worked out with Adam instead of him. He wondered why she felt the need to come sniffing around him again. Bigger game? "She'll be even more unhappy when she meets my fiancée."

His mother's tone turned to ice. "You know I'm very picky about who comes to the lake house."

"Yes," he said unable to stop a cruel smile. "I know. But once you meet her you'll love her as much as I do."

"I sincerely doubt it," his mother said then disconnected.

Doran's grin widened. *Good. I'm counting on it.*

Chapter Twelve

"I can't believe a month has gone by so fast," Ambrosia said as she helped Tanna pack while her daughter Hallie sat in the living room giggling over a video game she was playing in the living room.

Clothes lay neatly in piles on the bed—causal, formal and in-between—as the two women considered all possibilities. Doran was scheduled to pick her up in four hours.

"It has been an adventure," Tanna agreed not sure she was completely prepared for the big finale—three days with Doran's family. Fooling strangers had been easy, this would take more cunning.

"Will you miss him?" Ambrosia asked, inspecting one of Tanna's summer blouses before deciding to reject it and put it back in the closet.

"I'll miss the trips."

Ambrosia sent her a significant look. "Just the trips?"

"Do I need to mention Megan again?" She held up her ringed hand. "And this atrocity on my finger?"

"I think it looks good on you."

Tanna rolled her eyes. "He said the same thing. What is wrong with you two?"

"He said it looked good on you? You didn't tell me that."

"Because it wasn't important." She rested her hands on her hips then surveyed the clothes. "I think that's every-thing."

"You can admit it you know."

"Admit what?"

"That you'll miss him."

Tanna threw up her hands. "I just said—"

"That you'll miss the trips I know, but that's not the full story. I wouldn't blame you for falling for him just a little with all the gifts, traveling in a private jet to exotic places, the clothes and two weeks turned into almost four and then—"

"It's all a lie. I never once had a Cinderella moment. There's no clock striking twelve. I'm already a pumpkin, remember? That's the point. There's no happily-ever-after ending with this tale."

Ambrosia sighed. "I know, but you rearranged your schedule for him and if I were you—"

"You wouldn't have done this in the first place, remem-ber? You thought this was beneath me. That he was insult-ing me."

"I know but—"

Tanna held up three fingers. "Three more days. Let the countdown begin." She began to fold the clothes. After a few moments she realized her friend hadn't made a move to help her. She turned and saw Ambrosia with her arms folded looking at her. "What?"

"Don't under estimate your charm."

"What?"

Ambrosia took a step forward, her tone serious. "You keep talking about Megan, but why give him up so easily?"

"Because I don't want him."

"Why not help heal his broken heart?"

Tanna turned away from her and continued to pack. "I'm not interested."

"I don't know what it is, but there's something different about you since you met him. Before it was all about work, but you look younger and more carefree somehow."

"When a wealthy man takes you on trips around the globe as eye candy, you'd start to glow too. But after this weekend it's over and I'm going to forget all about him."

"But—"

Tanna threw down a roll of socks and glared at her. "I thought you were my friend."

"I am," Ambrosia said surprised by Tanna's tone.

"Then why are you trying to get my hopes up? Of course I'm a little attracted to him, but I'm not blind. I have more sense than to fall completely for a man like him. If he wasn't paying me to be by his side, he'd never look at me twice. I'm very aware that he chose me because I'm the exact opposite of the type of woman he'd be attracted to. So don't even hint at us being a couple again."

Ambrosia's eyes glistened with tears. "Tanna, I didn't mean—"

"I know," Tanna said with a quick smile to soften her words. "You look at me through the eyes of a friend who loves me. You don't see the flaws the world sees." She tilted her head towards the suitcase. "Now come on and help me get this over with."

She regretted her terse tone with Ambrosia, but she was angrier with herself because her friend had spoken as if she'd peered inside her heart. Tanna liked Doran more than she should. It was foolish to feel this way. He'd warned her and she'd heed his warning. Three more days. She'd count every minute like it was a prison sentence.

Any true feeling for him would cause her nothing but pain. She was just a prop to him, he was using her to pretend he was over his ex and to annoy his mother.

She had to keep that forefront in her mind. It didn't matter that when he'd first kissed her he'd made the world fade away, that the touch of his hand made her skin tingle, that she liked making him laugh. He was all charm and no heart. At least no heart to steal. Megan had it under lock and key and Tanna knew it. He was wounded and hurt, but in time if Megan wanted him, she could persuade him to come back to her.

No, falling for Doran would be crazy. He was totally off limits.

"Tanna, darling!"

Ambrosia and Tanna stared at each other frozen as they recognized the owner of the voice. What was her mother doing there?

"Tanna, I brought over some *egusi* for you! I'm putting it in the fridge."

"It's your mother," Ambrosia said, stating the obvious in a stage whisper.

Tanna quickly packed up the rest of her clothes, grimacing at the thought of them being wrinkled and crushed in her haste. Her mother couldn't see what she'd chosen or she'd start asking questions. "I know! How did she get in?"

Ambrosia briefly shut her eyes then said, "Hallie, come here!"

Moments later her daughter showed up in the doorway. "Yes, Mom?"

"Did you let Mrs. Ariyo in?"

"Yes."

"What have I told you about opening the door to strangers?"

"But she isn't a stranger."

Ambrosia blinked, not having a ready reply to that. "Never mind. Go back and play."

"Tanna," Mrs. Ariyo shouted from another room. "Why is your fridge so bare!"

"Coming Mum!"

"Have you not been eating? Oh my poor baby."

"I'll be right there."

But Mrs. Ariyo couldn't wait, she walked into Tanna's bedroom just as Ambrosia jumped on top of the suitcase.

She sent the two women a curious glance. "What are you two doing?"

"Just getting ready for my trip," Tanna said. "I leave in a few hours," she said, hoping her mother would understand the urgency.

But Mrs. Ariyo didn't appear to be in a rush. "You've been very busy this month."

"Yes, well...I like to be kept busy."

She studied the suitcase. "It looks quite big. Where are you going?"

"Slowly insane?"

Her mother frowned. "It wasn't funny the first time you said it."

"I told you. Just a weekend trip away to refresh my mind."

"And yet you won't tell me where you're going. Are you afraid I'll follow you?"

Tanna smiled. "It's crossed my mind."

Mrs. Ariyo made a motion with her hand as if gesturing Tanna closer. "If your aunt were here, she'd put a halt to that quick mouth of yours."

"I'm just teasing."

"Well, I'll let it pass because I have to ruin your plans."

Tanna paused, her stomach clenching. "What?"

"You'll have to go on this trip another time."

"But Mum, I can't—"

"I made a promise to Mrs. Layeni that I would help her clear up her daughter's room today. It's been three years since her passing and she's finally ready to put her daughter's things away. I wanted to help her, but then I realized that I also promised to be at the Lee's christening. It's the first child and it's important so I told Mrs. Layeni that you'd help her instead. You should have heard the joy in her voice. She's looking forward to it. You're always so comforting and it's been so hard for her."

Tanna gripped her hands feeling miserable. "I can't."

"She's been so unhappy these last few years and you always lift her spirits. She actually finds you funny and you make her smile when few things do. That's why I knew you were the best for her. I know you need your rest, but this would mean so much to her."

Tanna looked at Ambrosia silently pleading for help. Ambrosia shrugged her shoulders. Tanna sighed then looked at her mother again, calculating how much time she could spare. It wouldn't take her too long to get to Mrs. Layeni's place, quickly help her and then dash back.

"I'll do it, but I can only give her an hour," she said.

And at the same time, Ambrosia spoke up. "She's meeting a man, Aunty," she said using the respectful address for an older woman.

Mrs. Ariyo's eyes widened. "Really?"

Tanna spun around and mouthed 'Why did you say that?' before turning back to her mother. "No, it's—"

"You're meeting a man? Are you going off with him this weekend?" She playfully hit Tanna in the arm. "Why haven't we met him yet? Who is he?"

"It's nothing. Ambrosia is mistaken."

Mrs. Ariyo walked up to Ambrosia and nudged her off the suitcase. "What are you packing?"

Tanna rushed forward. "I'm all done now."

"No, you're not." Her mother gave her a hard shove towards the door. "You can go. I'll finish the rest for you."

"But—"

"You don't have much time. Mrs. Layeni will be waiting."

"Waiting?" her voice cracked.

"Yes, I told her you'd be there within the hour. Don't look at me like that, you're usually not busy, although you have been of late and now I know why. So you can explain that you can't stay long once you're there. When you come back I'll have everything ready for you and leave it by the door. It's the least I can do."

Tanna looked at Ambrosia who stared back at her helplessly. It was a battle she wouldn't win and she did want to help Mrs. Layeni. Hopefully, by the time she returned she'd be able to undo whatever choice her mother made. "I'll only do this once," she said then turned and left but not before hearing her mother say to Ambrosia, "Tell me all that you know."

Chapter Thirteen

"I didn't tell her anything," Ambrosia assured Tanna when she called her after finally escaping the Layeni house. She'd spent a lot longer—nearly three hours!—helping Mrs. Layeni pack away her daughter's things in a respectful way. Helping her decide on what to keep and what to donate. It had been heart wrenching seeing the images of the bright smiling face of the twenty-four year old her parents kept proudly displayed who'd met the wrong boyfriend. A twenty-six year old who'd killed her when she'd tried to breakup with him.

Tanna had listened to Mrs. Layeni's stories of her only daughter, at times fighting back her own tears. She tried to move quickly and efficiently rather than hurried, so that Mrs. Layeni wouldn't feel rushed in her grief. Then she'd offered to feed her and Mr. Layeni joined them and had stories of his own that he wanted to share. Before Tanna knew it, she realized she had only an hour to get back home, change and be ready for when Doran would pick her up. But first she had to make sure Ambrosia hadn't ruined anything.

She gripped the steering wheel with both hands as she sped through a yellow light. "Why did you have to mention a man?"

"She wouldn't let you escape for any other reason."

"But what did you tell her?"

"That you were going to a business retreat and that there was a man there you hoped to impress."

"So she doesn't suspect a thing?"

"What could she possibly suspect? What mother would think that her daughter would take money from a stranger to pretend to be his fiancée so that he can annoy his mother and get back with his ex?"

"You don't need to put it that way."

"There's no other way to put it."

"How are the tests going for Hallie? Any news?"

"No, we're still waiting for the results. Hopefully we'll hear this coming Monday."

"Ah, another reason I can't wait for this weekend to be over." She turned the corner and saw Doran waiting in the parking lot of her apartment complex, staring down at something on his phone. He wore dark shades, a black jacket and dark jeans looking like a model in a luxury car ad. She could imagine the voiceover saying, 'This is what power looks like.' Her foolish heart leapt at the sight of him. She would miss him even though she still didn't know him well. It was better that way. She could no sooner get close to him than cross the Grand Canyon in one leap. "He's here," she told her friend. "I've gotta go."

"Just wait."

"What?"

"If you get even the smallest chance, take it."

Tanna scowled and disconnected. Sometimes Ambrosia could push too hard. Dream too much. Tanna drove her car into a parking space a few cars away then raced over to him. He looked up when he saw her

"Sorry I'm late," they both said at the same time.

"What?" they echoed. "I said—"

They both stopped then Doran pointed to her signaling that she should go first.

"An emergency came up."

He tucked his phone away. "Same here."

"I'm glad. Whew," Tanna said making a gesture of wiping her brow. Although she really was sweating. She'd parked farther away from him than she'd thought and she didn't know how he could wear a jacket when she felt like the summer sun was hot enough to cook the black asphalt. "I'd hate to think I'd kept you waiting."

He shrugged. "I don't mind. A woman should always think she's worth waiting for."

"Oh," Tanna said, not knowing how to reply. Did he like waiting for Megan? She probably turned it into an art form. But she didn't like wasting time. "I'll be right back."

He grabbed her arm. "Slow down."

"But you said we needed to be on the road by—"

He kept his hand on her arm and started to walk, forcing her to follow his pace. "I know what I said. I just don't think you need to sweat more than you already are."

Tanna's face burned as proof that there was no chance between them slapped her in the face. How could he mention her sweaty face like that? She knew she looked a sight, but she'd just helped the Layenis move boxes of their daughter's beloved hardcover art books that seemed to weigh a ton each. She'd also helped them take out the bed and dresser. But it didn't matter. She tried to pull her arm free as they approached the front entrance to her apartment. "You don't have to follow me."

He tightened his grip. "I'll help you with your bags," he said, then opened the front door for her.

"Thanks," Tanna said, wishing she could close it in his face. She'd wanted to take a quick shower and change before seeing him again, maybe even refresh her makeup even though he wouldn't notice. She inwardly groaned; she wouldn't have time to repack. Fortunately, she didn't think whatever her mother had packed would make much difference, his mother still wouldn't approve of her no matter what she wore.

As her mother had promised, Tanna saw her suitcase ready near the door. Tanna dropped her handbag and keys on the couch then hurried towards her bedroom. "I won't be a minute."

"Tanna, I said—"

"I know, you don't mind waiting. That doesn't matter." She pointed towards the kitchen. "If you need anything to drink I think there's juice and some malt."

Doran took a seat. "I'm fine."

But she wasn't. She didn't feel comfortable having him in her place. Would his gaze skim over the handcrafted, hardwood furniture and oriental rug and only notice the wood carvings and large painting of a man playing a talking drum? Or would he also notice the iron work on the side table that she'd picked up in Iceland on her trip to see the Aurora Borealis?

Why did she care what he thought? Tanna chided herself as she quickly washed up, before she slipped into a fresh pair of jeans and loose green blouse. He likely wouldn't notice anything accept that she no longer looked like a melting chocolate bar.

"Okay, I'm ready," she said, heading to the door. She stopped surprised not to see him where she'd left him—sitting on the couch—but instead standing by a table, looking at the picture of her in the park with her one year old niece and nephew.

He pointed at the picture. "Was it as you predicted?"

She frowned. "Predicted?"

"Yes, did your sisters get pregnant at the same time?"

He remembered that? "Yes," Tanna said with a laugh, wondering what else she'd shared with him. Clearly too much. "And they're a joy," she said feeling silly. What else would she say?

"So are—" He began.

"I'm ready to go," she said at the same time. "Don't want to be late." She paused when she saw his expression change and realized she'd interrupted him again. She briefly closed her eyes. Why did she keep doing that with him? "I'm sorry. What were you going to say?"

His jaw twitch. "Nothing important."

She pressed her hands together. "I didn't mean it. I just have a lot on my mind. Please don't be angry."

"I'm not angry," he said then headed towards the hall.

"Where are you going?"

He gestured down the hall. "To get your other bags."

"What other bags?"

Doran glanced at her suitcase, stunned. "Is that it?"

"You said it was only for a weekend."

"I know but my sister takes a traveler's trunk with her wherever she goes. And I once had a girlfriend who never travelled with less than three bags."

"You've traveled with me before, when have I ever had a lot of bags?"

"I thought this weekend would be different. I thought you'd want to put on more of a show."

"Okay, wait a minute," Tanna said then disappeared and returned with two more suitcases of smaller size. "Is this better?"

He grinned. "Yes, that's more like it." He picked up the suitcases with more force than needed and stumbled back. He stared at her. "They're empty."

"Of course they're empty. I didn't have time to fill them. It's just for show. If you want, I can pretend that they're heavy." Tanna made a face and feigned struggling to lift one of the bags.

A quick grin touched the corner of his mouth. "Forget it, you won't be carrying it anyway and it will just confuse staff. We'll go with the one suitcase." He lifted her luggage and left.

"Is there anything else I need to know?" Tanna asked once they were on the road.

"No. Just follow my lead."

"I like to be prepared."

"Your job is easy. Just pretend to be completely in love with me." A vicious grin spread on his face. "Is that really so hard?"

"When you smile at me like that, yes it is."

His grin faded. "What's wrong with my smile?"

"Aside from its sadistic tinge?"

"I'm hardly a sadist."

Tanna glanced down at her engagement ring and said with a note of innocence, "What's this trip all about again?" she asked, knowing how much he'd enjoy irritating his mother. She fluttered her eyes at him. "I forgot."

He pulled the car over to the side of the road and parked. "Then let me remind you," he said in a deep tone then claimed her lips with his, shattering her resolve to keep him out of her heart. He hadn't kissed her like this since...

She pushed him away. "What are you doing?"

"Addressing your memory lapse."

"You didn't need to. You know I was just joking."

"I had to make sure."

"By wasting three kisses?"

"I didn't waste three. That was one long kiss."

"No, it wasn't. Every pause was a separate kiss."

He shook his head. "No, this." He bent down and placed a kiss on her neck, his lips hot against her skin. "And this." He placed another kiss further down. "Is a separate kiss."

She fought to keep her composure, although a passionate longing simmered within. "You're wasting your kissing quota," she managed to say, trying her best to meet his compelling gaze without melting.

"No," he said with a smile. A smile that this time was more of a predatory challenge than vicious. "I'm making a point."

"I think it's better you make your points when we have an audience."

"I'm only clarifying a few details. I thought you liked being prepared."

"I'm fully prepared now," Tanna said, leaning back, wishing he'd do the same. Why was he acting this way? Didn't he trust her? "Don't worry. I'll play my role well."

He stared at her for a long moment, but he still wore his shades so she couldn't see his eyes clearly. "I know." He drew back and started the car. "That's not what worries me."

Chapter Fourteen

I f he didn't know better, he'd think Tanna was eager to get rid of him. What was so wrong with his company? Sure, he'd taken up more of her time than he'd planned, but he treated her well. Most women would have been glad.

He sighed. The day wasn't a good one. It already hadn't started out as he'd hoped when he'd gotten a phone call from Rosemarie.

"He's here and I need you to do something," she said before she disconnected. Doran didn't have to ask who 'he' was and his sister wouldn't give him the option to refuse her summons. She opened the door just as he parked. "I thought you'd already be at the lake house," he said, stepping out of his car.

"I'm driving there later today."

Doran scanned the front yard. "Where is he?"

"In the sitting room."

He turned to her alarmed. "You let him in the house?"

"Of course."

"Why?"

"Because of this ridiculous inconvenience called 'neighbors'."

"And I'll assume that's also the reason you didn't call the police?"

She patted his cheek. "Clever boy."

He walked past her into the house. "This is the final time. Call Dillon next time."

"I did. He wasn't available."

Doran gritted his teeth. He'd walked into that one. Of course she'd call Dillon first. Everyone did. He was the sensible, smart one. People only called on him when they'd run out of options. Doran walked into the sitting room then swore. "It's empty."

Rosemarie came up behind him. "He was here a minute ago."

They heard something crash in the kitchen. Rosemarie marched in that direction. "If he ruins the new finish on the countertop, I'll kill him."

They found her ex-husband on the floor in front of the fridge, crying, a broken plate on the ground beside him. "I don't know why you won't give me another chance," he wailed. At six foot one, a touch of grey in his goatee, wearing a pair of crumbled khakis and an orange shirt that could use a wash and an iron, he made a pitiful sight.

Doran grabbed his arm and lifted him to his feet. "It's time to sober up."

Kelvin yanked his arm away and stumbled back. "I'm not drunk." He held out his hands. "I'm a man in agony," he said, then slid to the floor again and started to cry.

It had taken Doran fifteen minutes to finally get him to stop crying, when he was able to get him to his feet, he was seeing his way to victory. That was until Kelvin's mother arrived. A woman who blamed Rosemarie for her son's sorry state. A woman who'd gotten more out of the marriage—family trips, gifts, social connections—than her son had. She was just as eager to see the two reunited. And soon both mother and son sat on Rosemarie's couch crying. Another hour passed before Doran was able to convince them to leave.

And as he drove to Tanna's place he felt oddly excited to see her. But she hardly wanted to give him the time of day. He felt like an appointment in her business roster. And then she said she didn't like his smile.

It shouldn't have bothered him but it did. He'd worked very hard so that Tanna didn't see any of his eccentricities as Megan liked to call them. He'd treated Tanna the best he'd ever treated a woman. What was not to like? Sure, the plan against his mother was devious, but he wasn't being cruel. Once Tanna met her, she'd know that was an impossibility.

He hadn't meant to kiss her like that. He'd meant to tease her a little, but something came over him the moment his lips touched that tempting mouth of hers. After dealing with Rosemarie, Kelvin and his mother, Doran had felt tired, but somehow being with Tanna invigorated him. Kissing her, holding her close, invigorated him more.

Tasting her lips, tasting her tongue, tasting her skin, filled him with an insatiable hunger. Yes, it wounded his pride a little that she didn't desire him as so many others did, but his desire for her wasn't just because she was a challenge. He wasn't quite sure where the desire came from, just that it was there—simmering below the surface, threatening to consume him. He had to keep it at bay. He'd lost his heart once with disastrous results. He wasn't doing that again.

Especially with a woman who made it clear she had better things to do.

"So what was your emergency?" she asked him.

"Emergency?"

"Yes, the reason why you were late."

He wasn't in the mood to discuss Rosemarie and her ex. Having Tanna meet his mother would be enough, she didn't need to know about the loser his sister had married. "Car troubles."

"Oh, that's better than mine," she said then commenced to tell him about her family friends' loss. And he felt himself being drawn in. He knew she was kind, but hearing the compassionate way she talked about the couple, touched his heart. He gritted his teeth. Megan had been kind too. She'd donated hours of her time to a literacy group. It didn't mean anything.

But as Tanna spoke, Doran couldn't help noticing how the sun's rays caressed her skin, polishing the perfect surface of her face, the smooth curves of her bare arms, and swept across her chest, his gaze briefly lingering on the circular dip of her neckline leaving much to his imagination. He softly swore.

"Okay, fine," Tanna said sounding a little hurt. "I'll stop talking. I was just trying to fill up the silence."

"I don't mind you talking."

"Then why did you swear?"

He swore again this time silently. He hadn't meant for her to hear him. "No, it's not you. I was just…my sister's ex came by."

Tanna's eyes grew wide and she stiffened in her seat. "Tell me he didn't put another hole in the wall."

He glanced at her startled. "You saw those?"

"Of course, how could I miss them? I staged her house, remember? There are no secrets a house can hide from me."

For some reason, what she said helped him to relax. She knew about his sister's marriage and didn't care. He felt no judgment in her tone. "No, Kelvin didn't do any major damage this time."

"Did he break anything?"

Doran thought for a moment. "Just a plate."

She cringed. "The set on the table in the kitchen? Or the one in the dining room?"

Hell, he didn't know. He hadn't paid attention where the plate came from. "The kitchen," he guessed.

"Damn, I chose that set particularly. I'll have to see if I can get a replacement." She pulled out her cell phone and made a note. "Is that the only damage?"

"Aside from my shirt?"

"Your shirt?"

"Yes, his mother was equally upset."

"His mother was there?"

"Yes."

"And cried on your shoulder?"

He nodded.

"Lipstick, mascara or foundation?"

"What?"

"The stain. Which one was it?"

"I honestly don't know. It's the dry cleaner's problem now."

She patted his leg. "You're a good brother. I'm sure Rosemarie is very grateful."

His brows shot up. "You met my sister, right? I can't remember the last time she was grateful for anything."

"She was pleased with my work," Tanna said with a smug grin.

Doran scowled. "A rare exception."

Tanna couldn't help a giggle. "I know."

A smile tugged at his mouth. "So she gave you trouble too, huh?"

"Not too much."

He didn't believe her. "After helping her ex and his mother do you know what my sister did?"

Tanna shook her head.

"Go on. Guess."

Tanna bit her lip and scratched the side of her head. "Rosemarie. Rosemarie. What would she do?" She snapped her fingers as a thought came to her. "I bet you she was annoyed that you took so long to get rid of them."

He pounded the steering wheel amazed at her accuracy. "That's it!"

Tanna laughed. "I know. Your sister is…Oh, the stories I could tell you."

Doran tapped his ear, his mood lifting. "I'm listening."

"I can't."

"Why not?"

"It wouldn't be professional."

"Just one juicy little story. I promise I won't use it against her." He shook his head. "Forget it. I couldn't promise you that."

"See? That's why I won't tell you. It wouldn't be fair."

"But it would be fun."

"No."

He playfully pinched her cheek. "You're such a good girl."

She swatted his hand away. "Not always."

Doran felt his pulse quicken and when he spoke, his voice had a husky tone he couldn't hide. "That's good to hear."

Chapter Fifteen

Tanna had always thought cobras were beautiful and majestic creatures. Of course she'd never imagined them wearing dark purple lipstick and heels.

Vanessa Gibson looked like the kind of woman who'd scheduled the birth of her children between luncheons and delivered them without breaking a sweat. She had a cold, dangerous beauty. Tanna half expected the woman to test the air with her tongue.

"My God," Vanessa said, greeting them in the foyer. "You actually brought her here in that condition. When is she due?"

Tanna paused recognizing the insult—not only was she calling her fat, but she didn't have the decency to address her as anything else but 'she'—but didn't know how to respond. Did Doran want her to pretend she was pregnant? That would really rankle her. Or did he want her to become outraged and throw back an insult? Or perhaps he wanted her to laugh and turn it into a joke? Before she could decide he said, "She isn't pregnant, Mom."

His mother rested a hand on her chest. "Thank heavens for that."

"But it isn't from lack of trying."

His mother's hand fell to her side. "You can't even commit to the family business, I doubt you're ready to be a father."

"What I plan on becoming is none of your business."

Tanna cleared her throat. "It's a pleasure to meet you, Mrs. Gibson."

"You lie beautifully, but it won't help." She gave her a once over. "You really shouldn't wear a blouse like that. It does nothing for your figure or rather lack thereof. I'm very annoyed how late you are. I was expecting you an hour ago. The snack I had prepared was ruined. Oh, and before I forget, you'll be in separate rooms. The only sounds you'll be making in bed are sounds of sleep." Her mobile rang. "Excuse me," she said before strolling away.

Tanna watched her in admiration. "Well that was fast. Three insults in less than thirty seconds. Or was it four?" She turned to the front door.

He grabbed her arm. "You can't run out on me now."

Tanna turned to him surprised. "Why would I do that?"

"You just had this strange expression on your face and then turned to leave."

"It's because I didn't get a proper look at the house when we first drove up."

He frowned. "What's wrong with it?"

"Nothing," she said in awe. "So far absolutely nothing. It's a house stager's heaven. Three floors of architectural majesty with cathedral ceiling and wood floors, nestled in a gorgeous cove. Is there a lakeside deck?"

"Of course."

"Brick patio?"

Doran folded his arms, amused by her interest. "With a stunning view of the lake."

Tanna wiped the side of her mouth. "I'm drooling, aren't I?"

He grinned. "Only a little, but you'll have to wait for the full tour."

Her face fell. "Why?"

He took her hand and headed for the stairs. "We have to deal with something more important."

"What's more important?"

He sent her a significant look. "Our sleeping arrangements."

Tanna watched Doran direct one of the staff to set her suitcase in his room. She stood by the wall not sure what to do. She knew he wanted to irritate his mother, but she wasn't sure this was the best tactic. Sharing a hotel suite or villa with him was one thing. A bedroom was another. They'd never been in such intimate, close quarters before. She didn't see a couch for him to sleep on and doubted he planned to sleep on the floor.

"I'm not sure this is a good idea," Tanna said, once the man who'd helped with the bags had left and closed the door. "Your mother said—"

"My mother says a lot of things and I ignore most of them with great pleasure."

Tanna shook her head. "Doran, I don't—"

"It's not a morals thing. She didn't mind when I had—never mind. I just won't have her change the rules when she didn't before."

He'd been here with Megan. They'd been together in this room. That made it worse. No, what made it worse was the thought of him in only his pajama bottoms lying in bed next to her. Not that she knew much more about him even after being with him for nearly a month. She noticed he had a strange habit of turning a doorknob three times before opening it and he liked to have his clothes laid out in a certain way, but she'd always been a casual observer from a distance. What did she care if he walked around only in a towel if he was in another room? What did it matter what nightgown she wore if he didn't see it? But this was too close. There was nowhere to hide. "I can't do this."

"Why not?"

"Where are you supposed to sleep? I can't have you sleeping in the closet no matter how big it is."

"I'm not sleeping in the closet."

Her eyes widened. "You're going to sleep on the floor?"

"No," Doran said losing patience. "I'm sleeping in the bed."

She pointed to herself, outraged. "You expect *me* to sleep on the floor?"

"Tanna, nobody is sleeping on the floor."

"Then where am I supposed to sleep?"

He sat on the bed. "Is it really that hard to figure out?"

No, it's what I've been afraid of. "But we've never shared a bed before."

"Stop standing over there like a wallflower." He patted the mattress. "It's pretty comfortable."

She folded her arms, looking like a prim Miss, but feeling like a wanton woman, imagining him kissing her like he had in the car, except his mouth would be wandering much further south. How could she sleep with the sound of his skin, whispering against the sheets; dream without the lingering scent of his skin invading her thoughts?

Doran stood and held out his hands. "Come on, Tanna. Relax. Nothing's going to happen. If I try to grope you in my sleep you can just slap me."

His hands. She hadn't even allowed herself to imagine what his hands could do. His beautiful, warm hands slipping under the covers and sliding seductively down her leg...She hugged her arms tighter. "It's weird."

"No, it's not. We're like brother and sister."

"Would you really share a bed with Rosemarie?"

A look of horror crossed his face. "You have a point." He shook his head. "But this is different. We're friends and nothing's going to happen."

"I like to sleep naked."

"No, you don't."

"What if I did?"

A wolf's grin spread across his face. "I wouldn't stop you."

Tanna threw up her hands. "This is not funny."

His face changed and grew serious. "You really don't want to share a bed with me?" He closed the distance between them and grabbed her arms, his eyes dark and searching. "Did I scare you?"

Her heart leapt to her throat. "Scare me?"

"In the car," he said with a note of regret. "Is that why you're acting like this?"

The car. Why did he have to remind her about the car? And that kiss. No, it was more than one kiss. It was a series of intoxicating, deliriously wonderful kisses and it was all a game to him, but to her it was too real. She briefly closed her eyes, touching her fingers to her forehead. "No," she said, finally able to meet his gaze. "I'd already forgotten about that."

He straightened and folded his arms. "I'd never hurt you."

"I know that."

"Then why is your hand shaking?"

"Because I'm nervous. We're so close to making this work and I don't want to ruin it, plus…what about Megan?"

He rested his hands on his hips, his tone flat. "What about her?"

"If we didn't share a room, when you see Megan, you'd have a chance to be alone with her."

His face hardened. "I'm not doing this because of her."

Oh sure. "Plans change."

"I only have one plan. And if I were doing this to prove something to Megan," he held up his hand, "which I'm not, then it will be more convincing to have you share my room, right?"

Tanna reluctantly nodded. "You have a point."

"And the fact that I plan to marry you, means I expect my mother to treat you as something other than a girlfriend she expects me to dump in a couple months."

"And that is another good point but—"

"And you are safe with me," he said as if stating a vow. "That is a promise."

Tanna felt her face burn, embarrassed that she'd made him feel that he had to make such a declaration. "I know, Doran—"

"Follow me." He left the room, walked down the hall then stopped at another door. "*This* was supposed to be your room. Go on and look inside."

When Tanna stepped into the room, she saw what he meant. "Oh, your mother is mean," she said looking around the bedroom that was nearly twice as small as his room. It was serviceable, but lacked the large windows and over-stuffed pillows that greeted her in Doran's room. She rubbed her hands together. She'd temper her lust as long as she had to. "I must make her pay for this."

He winked. "Now you're getting the picture."

Chapter Sixteen

"Do you like your room, Tanzania?" Vanessa asked as she, Tanna and Doran sat in the sitting room nibbling on the snack Vanessa had expected them to eat hours ago. Not that Tanna thought it was a snack or that it had taken much preparation. She wasn't sure if the plate was creating an optical illusion or if the crackers topped with either sliced hard boiled eggs, a few capers and drizzled with olive oil or those with brie, red pepper and avocado were really the size of a dime. Although they were colorfully and exquisitely decorated, the moment they hit her mouth they seemed to dissolve without the need for chewing. Doran sat beside her and hadn't touched a thing.

"My name is Tanna," she corrected, taking another bite, pleased to know that dinner wouldn't be too far away.

"It's not short for anything?"

"Nothing you'd be able to pronounce."

Vanessa shot her a look as cold as the Arctic. "I speak three languages. Let me decide."

"I'll let you hear my full name on our wedding day," she said, affectionately rubbing Doran's thigh. Doran's tight, muscular thigh. What did he do in his spare time? Lift tree trunks? She started to pull her hand away, but Doran covered her hand with his own trapping it in place.

"And she has a beautiful name," he said.

"Of course you would think so," Vanessa said. "Your standards aren't as high as mine."

Tanna made a small, ineffective motion to pull her hand free from his grasp. "But thank you for asking, I love our room."

"Our?" Vanessa turned to her son. "I thought I said—"

"You did and we don't care. And we'll continue not to care until we leave. Unless you want us to leave now."

"Tansy dear—"

Doran's eyes darkened. "Tanna."

"Will you excuse us?"

"She doesn't need to."

"She has to if I want to speak to you alone, which I do."

Tanna knew a command when she heard one. She jumped to her feet. "Okay."

Doran pulled her back down. "No, it's not okay."

She met his gaze and said between her teeth. "Yes, it is." She squeezed his hand in warning.

He squeezed her hand in return, his tone also low. "I like having you by my side. You know how much I miss you."

She squeezed his hand a little tighter. "I won't be far and you promised I could see more of the house."

He glanced down at their hands and a slow secretive smile touched his lips. "So I did." He kissed the back of her hand then nipped it gently with his teeth before letting her go.

She stared at him and made a noise between a gasp and a laugh. Had he just bitten her because she was abandoning him?

"You'd better go before I change my mind," he whispered.

She sprung to her feet. "Let me leave you two. I'm eager to stretch my legs after such a long drive and walk around a bit."

"Yes," Vanessa said. "The exercise would do you good. Perhaps you'd make it a habit."

"Perhaps," Tanna said with a bright smile, walking behind where Doran was sitting, "and maybe I'll stroll down to the lake, fall in and nearly drown."

Vanessa lifted a cracker. "Only nearly?"

"Yes." She bent over Doran and wrapped her arms around his neck with playful adoration. "I don't plan to let anything steal me away from his side," she said, then bit the tip of his earlobe, holding back a grin when she felt his body tense. "Bye darling," she whispered then walked out the side door.

She shivered once she reached outside even as the summer sun struck her. How could a woman like that be the owner of such a splendid house?

Tanna strolled down to the lake, looked across it and noticed a house for sale, knowing it wouldn't be on the market for long. She turned and walked around the Gibson house, then strolled along a woodsy path, where she saw a little cross made out of popsicle sticks. She glanced at her watch to see how much time had passed before she would have to do battle again.

When she thought Mrs. Gibson had had enough time to sink her teeth into her son, Tanna made her way back up to the house. She paused when she saw Doran leave and march towards the lake with a determined look. She'd never seen that expression on his face before, or seen him walk with such an arrogant, forceful stride. When had he changed? Instead of the jeans and T-shirt, he'd had on earlier, he wore dark trousers and a light blue shirt. And where was he rushing off to? She raced over to him and grabbed his arm. "Has she got you thinking about drowning yourself?"

He spun around. Tanna quickly released her hold and took a hasty step back. The man wasn't Doran. He looked like him—similar build, coloring, eyes, but his mouth was a little thinner, his brows a little thicker, his face a little rounder.

They shared the same physique, cheek and jaw line, but this man had softer, more approachable features. "I'm so sorry," she said, stammering over the words. "I thought you were Doran. I've been waiting out here for him. Do you know if your mother is finished with him yet?"

The man stared at her in a way that made her wonder if he was a little slow, which was fine. She'd be patient. "How rude of me. First I grab you like a crazy woman and then ask you questions without first introducing myself." She held out her hand and smiled at him. "I'm Tanna Ariyo, your brother's fiancée."

"Dillon," he said, offering her a nice, firm handshake and a voice that reminded her of warm biscuits.

"It's a pleasure to meet you."

He held onto her hand and continued to stare at her in an odd way. She cleared her throat. *Was there something on her face? Was he awkward with strangers?*

"Do you know if your brother is free?"

He blinked. "Free?"

"From your mother," she said slowly. Poor thing. Was language hard for him? He was such a beautiful man too. It didn't matter. She didn't want him to feel awkward. "I was just walking around the property. Your house is wonderful. Would you like to show me around or were you heading somewhere?"

"No, I mean, yes." He rubbed the back of his neck. "I'm sorry, but this is kinda of a shock."

"Meeting me?"

He nodded.

"I know," Tanna said with sympathy. "Don't be too upset with your brother, it happened faster than either of us expected, but I know we'll be very happy together." She leaned in and winked. "That's if your mother doesn't chew him up first." She paused. Perhaps that was too harsh. What if Dillon thought his mother was a saint? She waved her words away. "Forget I said that. No matter what your mother thinks, I hope you'll give me a chance. I know I'm not your brother's usual flavor of the month and will take getting used to."

Dillon shook his head. "It's not that. It's just—"

Tanna didn't get to hear the rest of his sentence. A soccer ball hit her on the back of the head with enough force that she fell forward like a felled tree.

Dillon swore and kneeled down beside her. "Are you okay?"

"What just happened?" she asked, gingerly touching her stinging nose. When she pulled her hand away she saw blood.

"Dammit you're bleeding."

"It's okay. I have tissues in my purse, which I don't have right now."

He quickly unbuttoned and removed his shirt, revealing a muscular chest. "We need to put pressure on it."

"No, it's okay," she said quickly when he bundled up his shirt and handed it to her. She waved it away. "I'm all right, really."

"You're not all right," he said, pushing her hand away and gently pressing the shirt against her nose. "This is my fault."

"How could it be your fault?" she asked, her voice muffled against the fabric.

A young boy of about seven ran up to them. He had soft brown eyes and pudgy cheeks, although the rest of him was rail thin. "Dad I'm sorry," he said sounding out of breath.

"Don't apologize to me," Dillon snapped. "Apologize to her."

The little boy looked at her with sad brown eyes. "I'm sorry, ma'am. I didn't mean to hit you, I swear."

Ma'am? Why did that American term make her feel so old? "Call me Aunty and don't worry about it."

"I thought I'd locked that ball away," Dillon said.

The boy hung his head. "I didn't think anyone would be out here."

"The last time you—"

"I know, I know, but I didn't mean to that time either."

"Go to your room, we'll talk later."

"What happened last time?" Tanna asked unable to stop her curiosity.

"He killed a squirrel," Dillon said when his son remained silent. "Knocked the sucker right out of the tree. It didn't know what hit it."

The boy pointed towards the wooded area. "We buried it right over there."

"So that's what that was," Tanna said remembering the little cross.

His eyes lit up. "You saw it?"

"Yes, a very dignified send off."

" Gran doesn't know about it."

"My lips are sealed," she said in a solemn tone.

" And that's why we agreed no balls at the lake house," Dillon said, sending his son a harsh look.

The boy hung his head. "I'm sorry."

"It's okay," Tanna reached out and squeezed the boy's arm in reassurance. Seeing his dejected posture broke her heart. "Really."

"I'm so sorry," he said with tears in his voice before he turned and ran.

Dillon shook his head as he watched his son trip and fall before making it inside the house. "If only his moth-er…" He stopped and turned to her. "Let me see if the bleeding has stopped," he said removing the shirt. "We'll need to get some ice on it to get the swelling to go down."

"Don't be too angry with him. I'm sure it's hard for him to see you with anyone but his mother. Kids tend to act out when they're feeling unsure. Maybe he saw me grab your hand and misinterpreted it. Are you widowed?"

He shook his head.

"Divorced?"

He nodded.

"How long?"

"Not long enough," he said with a weary sigh.

"I suspected as much."

A slow smile touched his mouth. "No, it's not what you think. When it comes to Raymond it truly was an accident. He's not jealous about the women I see. He's just accident-prone. The squirrel story is true. My son could aim for a big red barn and miss." Dillon pulled out his mobile. "Arthur get an ice pack ready, I'll meet you in the kitchen."

Tanna started to smile then winced. "You sound like you've done this before."

"Too many times to count," he said with a groan that made Tanna laugh. "You're lucky you're not here for me." He helped her to her feet then led her to the house. "My last girlfriend ended up with a black eye when Raymond opened the door just as she was walking down the hall."

"That's why doors should swing in and not out. How would he know she was coming?"

"She also sprained her ankle when he tripped into her on the stairs and caused her to fall."

"That's your fault."

His brows shot up. "My fault?"

"Yes, you were supposed to be there to catch her."

Dillon threw his head back and laughed. "Yes," he said holding the door open for her. "I guess you're right."

Tanna looked up at him liking the sound of his laughter. "And what's a black eye and a sprained ankle when you can spend time with a sweet boy?"

"You don't know he's sweet." Dillon led her to the kitchen where the requested ice pack waited with a First Aid kit and refreshments.

"I'm sure he has his father's genes."

Dillon pulled out a stool from underneath the kitchen island. "Yes, and it gets me into trouble."

"Trouble?"

His eyes met hers and his voice deepened. "I end up falling for the wrong women."

Tanna cleared her throat, feeling suddenly flustered. "Yes, well falling isn't what it's cracked up to be. Just look at me." She glanced down at his shirt and noticed the label. Her heart dropped. "Please tell me you didn't give me a thousand dollar shirt to use as a tissue."

He took the shirt from her. "You sound as if you don't think I can get another one." He gently placed the ice pack on her nose. "Now hold this in place and go to bed."

"Bed?"

"To rest."

"I bumped my nose, not my head."

He frowned. "But—"

She waved her hand in a dismissive gesture. "You're worrying too much. I'll just hold this a little bit longer and then I'll have a nice purple bruise to annoy your mother with."

Dillon closed his eyes as if in pain. "Oh, damn that's right. The party's tomorrow. She can't have you looking like this." He slapped the counter with the flat of his hand. "I know. We'll get a bandage and say you just got some work done. No one will bat an eyelash."

"Do you honestly think that's necessary?"

"No," he said in dry tone. "You could tell her, and everyone who asks, the truth. That my son hit you in the head with a ball and you—"

Tanna held out her hands. "Your idea is brilliant."

Dillon grinned and gave a mock bow. "Thank you."

Minutes later he had her nose bandaged to look like she'd gotten some cosemtic work done. He held up a mirror. "What do you think?"

"You're an artist, doctor," Tanna said, tilting her head as if looking at her bandage from different angles. "I can't wait to see what my new nose looks like."

"I'm sure it will look stellar. I am the best after all."

"I only go to the best," Tanna teased, resting her arm on the counter. She accidentally knocked one of the bandages to the ground and they both bent down to retrieve it, bumping heads.

"Are you and your son trying to give me a concussion?" Tanna said with a laugh, holding her forehead.

"No," Dillon said with a chuckle rubbing his own sore forehead.

Doran entered the room and looked at them. "What's so funny?"

Chapter Seventeen

Tanna looked up at Dillon. "Doctor, should I tell him or should you?"

"It was your decision," he said with a straight face. "So I think you should."

She clasped the mirror to her chest and took a step towards Doran. "After how your mother treated me, I didn't feel pretty anymore so I decided to get my nose done. I'll get my chin done next."

Doran folded his arms. "I don't like people having fun without me. What are you two up to?"

"She just met Raymond," Dillon said.

Doran blinked, swore and then rushed over to her, cupping her face in his hands, his eyes searching her face. "What did he do to you?" He glanced down at her body then met her gaze again. "Are your hurt anywhere else?"

For a moment, Tanna couldn't speak, surprised by his tender concern. He'd never looked at her like that before— as if she truly mattered to him. *I don't want you falling for me,* he'd warned her. She took a step back and let out a nervous laugh. "Your nephew hit me in the back of the head with a soccer ball. It was my fault for falling forward and smashing my nose. Fortunately, I'm all better now thanks to your brother."

Doran shoved his hands in his pockets, an expression she couldn't read closing over his features. "Good."

"And I bet, he's the older one so I was trying to get into his good graces in case I need him as an ally against the queen."

The brothers shared a look, but Doran turned away first and folded his arms. "Hmm."

Dillon patted Tanna lightly on the back. "You don't have to try any harder. I already like you. If you need anything, let me know."

"She'll be fine. I'm here now," Doran said.

"Right," Dillon said, the same poignant, secretive glance passing between them. "I'll go check on Raymond."

Doran waited for his brother to leave then looked at Tanna again, concern in his eyes. "Are you sure you're okay? You're not just putting on a brave face?"

Tanna tapped her chest with pride. "You're looking at a girl who survived five consecutive whacks from Aunt Violence."

He didn't smile.

She held up her hand, spreading out her fingers. "Did you hear me say five?"

He still didn't smile.

"That was supposed to be funny."

He turned away from her, leaned against the counter and unrolled one of the bandages then rolled it up again.

Tanna sighed and decided to change the subject. "I didn't know you had a twin."

"Hmm."

"How was the talk with your mother?" She looked him over. "I don't see any scars."

Doran patted his chest then unrolled the bandage again. "That's because they're all inside."

"Ah too bad. I can't kiss and make them better."

He rolled the bandage back up then turned to her and lifted his shirt. "Actually there are a few external ones."

Tanna leaned in closer to examine the beautiful column of skin he displayed and squinted, her fingers itching to touch him. "I don't see any."

"You have to look closer. Maybe if I took my shirt off—"

"That was your brother's idea," Tanna said quickly in her defense. "I didn't ask him to do it and even tried to stop him. It's the truth," she said when he looked doubtful. "Besides, he was only helping me to stop the bleeding."

"Yeah," Doran said in a sour tone, unrolling the bandage once more. "A real gentleman."

"I know you're not jealous." She lowered her voice. "So I'll guess you're worried that I broke my cover. You can be assured that I didn't. I only wanted to make sure he liked me."

"You succeeded." He rolled the bandage up. "You weren't supposed to get hurt."

"It was an accident. A *minor* accident."

"I said you'd be safe," he said unrolling the bandage with more vigor.

"I am safe." She covered his hand. "Will you cut that out?"

He took a deep breath. "I will, just let me finish."

"Finish?"

"I have to roll it back up."

The tone and look made it clear that he had to. She removed her hand and watched him roll the bandage back into place. He looked around the kitchen as if searching for something.

"What are you looking for?" she asked.

"I have to get this out of my sight or I'll start again."

"Give it to me and close your eyes."

He did.

She put the bandage on a stool hidden underneath the island. "Okay, you can open your eyes now."

He rubbed the knuckles of his fist. "I'm not crazy. I just—"

"You don't have to explain."

He rubbed his knuckles harder. "I should have warned you about Raymond."

"Not much you could have done. To be honest it was almost a relief. I'd already made an idiot of myself. I'd grabbed Dillon's arm thinking he was you at first then started rambling about something I can't remember now and then boom! I was on the ground. I went from one embarrassment to another, but I decided to look on the bright side. My nose hurts, but it's not broken and I don't have a headache. Besides, I was in good hands and your brother came up with a great story for the party tomorrow. Isn't that clever?"

Doran turned his gaze to one of the large bay windows, rubbing his fist even harder, and mumbled under his breath, "Of course, he's the smart one after all."

"What?"

"Nothing."

Tanna removed the bandage from its hiding place and put it on the counter. "Here. I prefer you toy with this than rub your hand as if you're trying to start a fire."

He shoved his hands in his pockets. "I'll stop." He nodded to the bandage before closing his eyes. "Put that away, but somewhere else since I now know where it was."

Tanna tossed the bandage under the kitchen table. She'd retrieve it later. "Okay."

He opened his eyes. "Thanks," he said, but his eyes looked sad. He reminded her of the man she'd found outside the castle looking lost. She knew the reason for his sadness back then, he'd suffered a broken heart, she could only imagine what his mother had said to put that expression on his face now.

She lightly touched his sleeve. "Could I get you a drink?"

The shadow of a smile touched his lips. "Maybe another time." He gently tore off the creative bandaging on her nose. "If the bruising is really bad tomorrow, we'll use makeup. You don't need this. You're fine just the way you are," he said in a soft voice.

"You too," Tanna said, wishing she could erase the sadness from his eyes. She jumped up and sat on one of the stools so that they were almost of equal height. "Do you know what's better than a drink?"

"What?"

She held out her arms. "A hug." She knew it was corny, but she'd do anything to lift his spirits, even a little. She hoped to make him smile, instead his gaze darkened and in one smooth motion his arms encircled her body and he clasped her body tightly to his.

Tanna swallowed, her mind racing as her hands felt the rope muscles of his back. His brother, half naked, didn't affect her as much as Doran did fully clothed. She briefly closed her eyes indulging in the luxurious pleasure of being so close to him. She should have offered to hug him before. Maybe he felt something too? Maybe his feelings towards her were beginning to change. The sound of footsteps hurrying into the kitchen dashed her hopes, pounding on her dreams with their cruel reality. He'd probably heard them coming before she did. All his actions were part of the pretense. None of it was real.

The sound of the footsteps stopped then a female voice behind Tanna said, "Your brother told me to clear up the First Aid kit and make a new ice pack."

"We'll take care of it," Doran said. But even as the footsteps faded he didn't let her go, and she wasn't sure if she imagined it or if he had really held her a little tighter before finally stepping back and releasing her. "It's not better than a drink, but it will hold me for a while."

"Until the next round?"

"Don't worry," he said, the look of sadness gone from his gaze, replaced by a mischievous glint. "I'm fully prepared for that."

Chapter Eighteen

illon didn't realize he was whistling as he walked to his son's bedroom. *So that was the woman his brother planned to marry?* She wasn't like any of the others his brother had paraded in front of him before. She was pretty, not as striking as the women his brother usually chose, but her big brown eyes and bright smile made up for a lack of perfection. He liked her laugh and how she hadn't gotten angry at Raymond.

His good mood fell. *Raymond.* He had to deal with him and wasn't sure how.

He took a deep breath before he walked into his son's room and found Raymond sitting on his bed with his legs drawn up, pressed against his chest. "I didn't mean to hurt her," he said in a small voice. "Is she really angry?"

Dillon sat on the bed. "No. Why did you disobey me?"

"I'm always picked last for gym and I thought if I got better with my kicking that maybe they'd choose me."

"You could have told me that."

"You're always busy."

"I would have made time."

"I don't like when you get mad."

Dillon sighed. He did get impatient with Raymond. It was hard having such a clumsy son. But he tried his best not to show it. As a kid, Dillon had succeeded at every sport he chose, his son tripped over his own shoes and was as coordinated as a drunk octopus. "I'm sorry. I'm not mad at you I just want—"

"Me to be better," Raymond finished. "I wish I was better. I wish I wasn't so stupid. Gran says I'm useless."

Dillon rested his hand on his son's head, taking control of his temper. His mother had a wicked tongue and it hadn't softened with age. It had only gotten worse. He'd never been the object of her criticisms, he'd worked too hard to please her. His brother, on the other hand, had gotten the brunt of it, leaving little left for him to deal with. Now his mother had set her sights on his son who, unlike Doran, took every cruel remark to heart. "You're not stupid or useless," he said, wondering how often he'd have to say those words so that his son would believe them, "and you will get better. I'll help you with the soccer later. Okay?"

Raymond nodded, opened his mouth then closed it.

"What?"

"That woman, is she really going to marry Uncle Doran?"

"It looks that way," he said, still surprised his brother was ready to settle down with a woman so opposite his usual type.

"I'm glad. I didn't like the other ones."

"They each had their own charm," he said determined to be diplomatic.

"I like her."

Dillon sighed again, remembering Tanna's laughter and smile. "Me too."

It wouldn't work. Whatever that conniving, disobedient son of hers was up to, it wouldn't work. She wouldn't let it.

Vanessa lay on her massage table as the masseuse kneaded her muscles. She was tight. Too tight. How dare he! And at such an important time. The irritating little brat. What did he think he was doing? How could he just look at her as if nothing she said mattered?

"You're really tense today, ma'am," the masseuse said, a lanky woman with big hands. Vanessa could imagine her cracking walnuts with her thumbs.

Tense? She thought she was tense? *I know that you idiot, why do you think you're here?* "It's been a trying day."

"Are you doing the breathing exercises we'd discussed?"

Was the child actually lecturing her? She'd have her replaced tomorrow. "Hmm."

"If you—"

"Let me explain something that you're forgetting. I ask the questions, not you. Understood?"

"Yes, ma'am."

Vanessa took a deep, steadying breath, but could still feel the beginnings of a headache. To think that tomorrow she'd have to introduce that woman—such a woman!—as a potential daughter-in-law. No, she wouldn't. If she had to introduce her at all she'd refer to her as her son's friend. But he seemed bent on ruining things. Even though he'd treated her with such nonchalance when she'd finally gotten him alone.

"The Hayfields are coming and I'm hoping to have them invest in my foundation."

"I'm sure you'll succeed," Doran said sounding bored. "Is that what you wanted to talk to me about?"

"They like to see a stable, successful family," she said undaunted by his lack of interest.

He lifted a brow. "Are we supposed to find them one?"

"Megan will be there."

"So I've heard."

"It's your chance to tidy up whatever misunderstanding transpired between you two."

He trailed a finger along the arm of the couch. "There was no misunderstanding."

"If you would just tell me what happened, I could—"

"Nothing happened. It just ended."

"But you were—are so perfect for each other."

"I'm with Tanna now."

Vanessa rolled her eyes and bristled. "What a god awful name."

He waited.

"I'll never accept her."

"You haven't given her a chance."

"She has a degree in what?"

"She's a home stager. You should see what she did with Rosemarie's place."

"A man in your position needs someone who will—"

"I'm not joining the company. You already have Rosemarie and Dillon at your beck n' call. I'm fine doing what I do."

"Yes," she said. She clasped her hands together and lean forward with feigned interest. "How is your little hair salon doing?"

"The three branches for my men's grooming business are doing very well."

Vanessa sat back disappointed, his jaw didn't even twitch this time, she must be losing her touch. She'd needle him another way. "I still can't believe you abandoned your family obligation for such a ridiculous venture."

"And it makes me a ridiculous amount of money."

She didn't know how he managed it. His greatest problem was that things came too easily to him. In school he was popular and well liked. He'd started making money even then. At fourteen a local store offered to give him free clothes because whenever he wore something other kids would follow. He later got paid, even though he didn't need the money "I'm worth it," she remembered him telling her one day when she saw him counting his money. He eventually went into business with the store owner and it expanded into his men's grooming business. She'd thought it was a passing phase. She didn't think it would become so lucrative since he was so careless when it came to business. He'd gotten lucky in the partner he'd chosen.

But choosing a wife was something else entirely. Soon he'd get tired of his rebelliousness and join the company, but to start a family with such a woman. A woman with a face as wide as a plate and skin as dark as a raisin…no. A woman like Tanna was everything she couldn't stand. One of those unsophisticated, upstart immigrants who came and stole jobs other scrambled for. Her family had struggled and built a life in this country after being brought in chains from Ghana. Theres was a proud heritage of betrayal, sacrifice and victory. What would someone like her know about their history? Their heritage? Their traditions?

Megan understood the subtle, important nuances of their culture. Tanna had no such finesse. And that figure. How could a woman let her body go like that? Did she have no shame? Vanessa closed her eyes. If her husband was still around he could advise her. Doran always seemed to listen to him more. He was being stubborn, but she'd find a way to change his mind.

But a least she'd had one minor triumph, Vanessa thought when she recalled the small surprise she'd sprung on Doran.

"Are we finished now?" he asked, beginning to stand. "I told Tanna I'd give her a tour."

"In a moment. Someone wants to see you first."

His face changed and for a moment he looked like a trapped animal. "You didn't."

Vanessa didn't know what had given her away, how he could have guessed at her surprise since he wasn't the brightest, but he had. She smiled, pleased to see the look of boredom and smug defiance wiped from his face. "She wanted to drop something off before the party. I said she could."

Doran jumped to his feet, but it was too late. Megan walked into the room. "Hello, Doran," she said, saying his name with an intimacy that was telling.

Vanessa remembered the look on his face—shock, mingled with fear and hurt. A beautiful combination.

Shock she'd expected. Fear had its place, but the hurt. She smiled at the memory. The hurt in his eyes was just the ammunition she needed. Hurt was good. Pain she could use. It was one of the few ways she could manipulate him.

He still felt something for Megan, he could deny it with his mouth, but it was clear in his face and the feeling was strong.

Vanessa felt her muscles relax. She didn't care that Doran had given Megan curt replies to her questions or that he'd cut their conversation short before storming out of the room.

"Are you sure this is a good idea?" Megan had asked her. "I'm not sure this will work."

"Just do as we discussed and everything will be fine."

And she knew it would be. Doran still loved Megan. She planned to use that to her advantage.

Chapter Nineteen

He'd run right into her pitchfork.

Doran sat on the edge of the pier and stared over the still lake waters, the fading light of the summer evening slowly settled around him, the waning sunlight cascading over the waters. He'd left Tanna alone after dinner to give her time to get used to their new sleeping arrangements. He was beginning to wonder about them himself, but he'd handle that later.

Right now he had to think.

He should have been more prepared. He should have expected his mother would have something up her sleeve. If he had been more on guard she wouldn't have caught him unaware and hit his soft spot. What shocked him the most was that he still had one. The strength of his feelings at seeing Megan again nearly toppled him. His heart cracking and bleeding all over again as she spoke to him. He stared at her, angered that she could still affect him.

He didn't even remember what he said before he left. It didn't matter anyway, his mother had won that round. And that kind of triumph would make her bolder. He'd planned to tell Tanna that she had to be careful, then heard her laughter. When he walked into the kitchen and saw her with his identical twin brother—his *shirtless* twin brother—fury almost choked him.

Tanna was his.

Dillon could have his mother's praise and love. He easily escaped her wrath. His brother could have Rosemarie's respect and the admiration of all the employees of their family's business.

He could not have Tanna, even in a small way.

Although it was just pretend, he wanted all of Tanna's attention, her smiles and her laughter. He wanted her to think he was smart. He wanted to be the one she turned to.

Doran gritted his teeth. But he hadn't gotten that chance. He hadn't been there when she'd gotten hurt, instead Dillon had come to the rescue, cared for her and made her laugh.

He gripped his hand into a fist. He wasn't falling for her. He was still raw from seeing Megan again and that had made him vulnerable.

No, he wasn't falling for her. When he fell, he fell hard and he wasn't going to do that again. He'd been burned once, twice would be stupid. And he wasn't stupid.

It wasn't his fault she was so likable, right? There was no harm in liking her a little bit. He couldn't have come this far in their plan otherwise. And was it his fault that she seemed to say just what he needed to hear?

He probably shouldn't have hugged her. Kissing her was one thing, but hugging her…hugging her brought out a craving he'd long kept buried. Feeling the soft give of her breasts against his chest, feeling the warmth of her body pressed against him. Holding her in his arms, he forgot about his mother and Megan.

That's what shook him the most. For one wild moment, Megan meant nothing. His cracked heart became whole once more and he felt as if he could achieve anything. He felt renewed, as if he could do battle with his mother and win.

Doran leaned back on his elbows and stared up at the sky as the silhouette of a flock of birds soared overhead. A soft smile spread on his face.

No, he probably shouldn't have hugged Tanna. Sleeping close to her tonight would be a challenge and he'd have to fight hard to stay on his side of the bed, but he wouldn't change a thing.

Chapter Twenty

She was starving. Was that grassy stack of greens supposed to be dinner? True, the large mandarin salad was beautifully made, but after finishing it she was so hungry she could have eaten the plate. Fortunately, she'd been left alone and planned to do something about it. Doran had disappeared somewhere upstairs, Dillon and Raymond were in the TV room and Mrs. Gibson had slithered into her den early.

With the delight of a child on the hunt of a cookie jar, Tanna tiptoed into the kitchen and opened the fridge, hoping to find something—anything!—that would make her feel full.

"What are you looking for?" Dillon asked, Raymond following shyly behind him.

She froze. Caught! She let her shoulders drop. No use denying it. "Food."

"Dinner wasn't enough?"

"I don't know why you even use utensils. You might as well just swallow air."

He grinned. "You're in luck, I brought a secret stash." He opened up the freezer.

Her mouth dropped when she saw the carton. "Ice cream," she said in awe. "Do you have cones?"

He opened up a cupboard, pushed some boxes aside and pulled another to the front.

"My savior," Tanna said wanting to hug him. "I don't suppose you'd have caramel, colored sprinkles and a cherry, too?"

"That's asking too much."

"Then I'll improvise." She saw a jar of nuts then looked at Raymond as if he were a coconspirator. "How would you like a nut covered ice cream cone?"

He nodded and climbed up on one of the stools.

She grabbed the cuttingboard and chopped up some nuts, rolled the ice cream in it then handed it to him. "There you go," she said with a flourish.

"Thank you," he said, his voice eager. He took one lick and the scoop of ice cream toppled to the ground with a splat.

His shoulders fell.

"You know what?" Tanna said, quickly snatching up the ice cream and throwing it away. "I've always thought milkshakes were sooo much better." She looked at Dillon. "Don't you think so?"

His eyes twinkled. "Yes, much better."

She wiped her hands. "Let's have that instead."

She quickly chopped up some strawberries and bananas that were sitting in a bowl on the counter and made a milkshake then handed it to Raymond, holding her breath. He took it and drank it without incident.

"Good save," Dillon whispered as his son happily sipped his drink.

"I try." She handed him his glass.

Doran entered the room. "How come I keep finding you two alone in the kitchen?"

"We're not alone," Tanna said, nodding to Raymond.

"I had to see how my patient is doing," Dillon said.

Doran nodded at the drink in his brother's hand. "What is that?"

"We're having milkshakes," Raymond said, swinging his feet. "It's sooo good."

Doran walked over and stood beside Tanna. He shook his head. "If Mom catches you."

"It's worth it," Dillon said.

Doran took Tanna's glass just as she was about to drink. He took a sip. "Mmm not bad."

"I could have this every day," Raymond said.

Tanna reached for her glass. Doran moved it out of reach and kept drinking. "It's not good for you," he said.

"Yes it is. She used fresh berries and bananas. I saw her."

Tanna made a face at Doran then grabbed a small glass and filled it with the remnants of what was left in the blender and drank it—about three sips worth.

He finished his glass then set it down. "Thanks, honey." He kissed her, his lips cold from the drink.

Five, she mouthed when he drew away, making sure he knew he'd reached his limit of kisses. "My pleasure," she said through clenched teeth. "Although I didn't expect you to finish it all, dear."

"You can have some of mine," Dillon said.

She eagerly held out her glass. "Thank you."

Doran pulled her close to his side. "I'm sure there's no need for that."

Dillon noticed the possessive gesture with a smile. "If you hadn't been so greedy, you would have noticed that she was hungry."

"Then I'll help her make another one."

"Why make her go through all that trouble? Oh, I forgot your priorities always come ahead of others."

Doran's tone hardened. "She's a top priority to me."

Tanna waved her hand. "Still here in case you didn't notice."

The two brothers ignored her.

"You have a funny way of showing it," Dillon said.

"If she's really hungry, I'll take her somewhere."

"I don't want to go somewhere," Tanna said. "I just want a milkshake." She held her glass out to Dillon. "Thanks for the offer to share."

Doran took the glass from her. "I'll help you make another one."

"Can I help too?" Raymond said.

"Sure," Tanna said.

"No!" His father and uncle said in unison.

"You don't want him around sharp objects," Dillon said.

"The last time he tried to put something in the toaster it caught fire," Doran said.

"I'm sure it will be okay," Tanna said. "But I can't have you both standing there like that making him nervous. Scram."

Dillon shook his head. "Tanna, I don't—"

"We'll be fine."

He looked at his son. "You listen to everything she says, understood?"

"Yes, Dad."

He headed towards a cupboard. "The First Aid kit is—"

She pushed him towards the door. "Go."

Doran looked at Raymond then her. "You don't have to do this."

"Yes, I do. And if I get hurt…" She smiled and fluttered her lashes. "I can blame you."

"Where's Tanna and Raymond?" Rosemarie asked when her brothers joined her on the patio.

"In the kitchen," Dillon said, taking a seat. "She's showing him how to make a strawberry-banana milkshake."

Rosemarie blinked. "She's letting *him* help her?"

He nodded.

"She's a brave woman. Do you think she'll scream when she loses a finger?"

Dillon jumped to his feet. "Maybe I should check on her."

Rosemarie laughed and shook her head. "It was a joke. I'm sure she'll be fine."

Dillon sent a nervous look at the door. "You didn't see what he did to her this afternoon."

"Sit down, if anyone is supposed to be racing to her rescue it should be her fiancée." She shot Doran a look.

The silent rebuke didn't faze him. "Tanna doesn't need rescuing," he said.

She nodded. "Of course." A naughty grin quirked the corner of her mouth. "However, if she were Megan…" She let her words fade away, her challenge hanging in the air. When he didn't take the bait, she continued. "I heard she stopped by. Sorry I missed that reunion."

"Megan stopped by?" Dillon asked.

"Yes, Mom mentioned it." She looked at Doran. "How is she?"

"You'll see her tomorrow," Doran said. "Why are you asking me?"

"Oh dear, am I upsetting you?"

"Leave him alone," Dillon said. "I'd hate it if my ex showed up here too."

"Yes, but you're not still in love with her."

Doran rested his chin in his hands and gazed out at the water.

Dillon leaned back in his chair. "Neither is he."

"Maybe, but something improved Mom's mood at dinner and I don't think it was her massage."

"It wasn't Megan," Dillon said. "Doran's completely over."

"How do you know?"

Doran looked at his brother equally intrigued.

"Have you met Tanna yet?" Dillon asked her.

"Yes."

"Isn't she amazing? A breath of fresh air."

"Sure, but—"

Dillon nodded at his brother. "Go on and tell her."

"Tell her what?" Doran said confused.

Dillon looked at his sister. "She could tell us apart."

Doran stiffened; Rosemarie's gaze sharpened. "What did you just say?" she said.

"Tanna can tell us apart," he repeated emphasizing every word.

Rosemarie leaned forward with interest. "Are you sure?"

"Positive. She grabbed my arm then looked at my face and knew I wasn't Doran. You know what that means."

"Oh my God," Rosemarie said. "Doran you sly thing."

"Don't make a big deal out of this," Doran said.

Dillon frowned. "I thought you'd be happy."

Rosemarie sniffed. "What does he have to be happy about? It's not real." She lifted a brow at Doran, urging him to disagree. "Is it?"

Doran rubbed his chin.

Dillon looked at them both. "What's going on?"

"I think our little brother is trying to pull a con."

Doran stared off at something in the distance.

Dillon frowned at him. "What is she talking about?"

Rosemarie folded her arms. "Nothing. Just don't be surprised if our brother is suddenly free and single in a couple of months." Rosemarie swung her foot. "However, if Mom finds out that she can tell you apart that may change things."

"Mom's not going to find out anything," Doran said. "And you aren't going to mention it. I'm sure it was just luck. Her two younger sisters are twins, so perhaps she developed a knack."

"You know it's a big deal."

"No, it's not."

"I ignored the warnings and look what happened to me," Dillon said.

"Your marriage didn't break up because of some family myth."

"I'm not so sure any more." He shook his head confused. "Why are you fighting me on this? You can use this information as ammo against Mom. She tried to surprise you with Megan and you can blow her away with this. It will be hard to fight."

Doran stood. "I'm going to check on Tanna," he said before he left.

Dillon looked at his sister, baffled. "What's wrong with him?"

"You honestly don't see that this is all a lie?"

"What's a lie?"

"Tanna and Doran's engagement. I think he's using her to pass off as his fiancée so that the dragon will leave him alone."

Dillon shook his head. "No, it's real. When he's with her, he's different."

"Then why isn't she wearing one of the family rings? It's tradition to offer it during an engagement."

"You know Doran likes to break traditions. He's probably waiting to give it to her on their wedding day."

Rosemarie shook her head. "No, it's proof their relationship is not real."

"I think it is."

Rosemarie rubbed her hands together and smiled. "Wanna make a bet?"

"Sure. A hundred."

"Why so conservative?"

"Okay, two hundred."

"Why not a thousand? Unless you're not sure," she said her smile widening. "I wouldn't blame you for having some doubts."

"I don't. Let's make it fifteen hundred."

She held out her hand. "When you pay me, make sure it's cash."

Chapter Twenty-one

Doran walked into his bedroom then stopped when he saw Tanna lying on her side reading a book. She wore a long blue satin nightgown that swept over her generous curves, sending a subtle invitation. He gripped the doorframe, his body responding to her.

She sat up when she saw him, swinging her legs over the bed, giving him a brief glimpse of her dark chocolate legs before her nightgown covered them. He could picture slipping it from her shoulders and letting it fall to a puddle at her feet. Or better yet, he could slowly slide it up her legs, up her thighs, over her hips and…

He silently swore. If he stayed, he wasn't going to behave himself. He was too close to making his plan work to ruin things now. It didn't matter that he wanted to sink in-between her thighs with his tongue, with his hand, with his body. He wanted to find out if she was noisy or quiet. If she liked it slow or fast or somewhere in-between. Was she bossy or submissive? Did she like to be on top or below? He didn't care which, he'd let her ride him all night long and then switch places and take her to the moon and back.

"Are you really that surprised to see me all in one piece?" Tanna asked.

"What?"

"Why are you just standing there?"

Because I'm afraid to move. "Did you enjoy your milkshake?"

"Very much and Raymond was fun. Doran, are you sure something's not wrong? Did you have another meeting with your mother?"

Oh damn, she was standing and coming towards him with that look in her eyes. He could dive into those brown eyes of hers and drown with pleasure. If she offered to hug him, he wouldn't be able to control himself. No, he could, he wouldn't want to. He'd find out the answer to every question he had about her and then come up with more. He darted sideways and made a big arch away from her as he headed to his suitcase. "Nothing's wrong."

She folded her arms. "You don't have to avoid me."

"I'm not avoiding you," he said, opening his suitcase before remembering it was empty. Why did the staff have to be so efficient with putting things away?

"Then why are you acting as if I have something catching?"

Yes, he wanted to catch her and hold her and… "It's not that." He closed his suitcase. He needed to get out *now.* He took a deep breath and looked at her."I have some business I have to take care of."

"Is it bad? You look really worried."

He stepped back when she reached out to touch his sleeve. "It's nothing I can't handle." He shoved his hands in his pockets. "I'll see you later."

"Should I leave a light on?"

He headed for the door. "No, I'll find my way."

"I don't mind. I'd hate the thought of you groping your way through the dark."

Groping. That would be fun. "You're right, better keep a light on. Sleep tight," he said, then left knowing he wasn't going to sleep at all.

She'd worried for nothing. He hadn't even come to bed that night. She'd worn her longest, loosest nightgown to hide her traitorous body and it hadn't mattered at all. Where had he spent the night? What business had he needed to attend to? Was that real or an excuse? Did it matter?

Tanna showered and changed. She was in the bathroom putting her makeup on when she heard the bedroom door close. She came out and saw Doran sitting on the side of the bed wearing the same clothes he'd worn from yesterday, looking tired and disheveled. "Did you work all night?"

He jumped up when he saw her. "No."

"You look awful."

He rubbed his cheek. "I need to shave and shower." He rubbed his eyes. "Or is it shower and shave?"

"Were you up drinking?"

"No, but that probably would have been a good idea."
He stepped into the bathroom. "See you at breakfast," he
said, then closed the door.

The man would continue to be a mystery to her, but
that wasn't her problem. Today was an important day. The
day of the party. She could already hear movement outside
as the staff prepared for the festivities, and no cloud
darkened the sky as if Vanessa had ordered it to be so, but
first she had to survive breakfast with the family.

Except there was nothing to chew. Tanna stared at the
bowl of yellow-orange colored mush in front of her not
knowing what to make of it or the tall green drink that
stood beside it. She'd taken a sip and had to fight hard not
to gag at its bitterness.

"Excuse me," Tanna asked Dillon who sat beside her.
"What is this?"

"It's best not to ask," he said in a low voice.

"Yes," Raymond said on the other side of her. "Gran
will get mad."

Tanna looked up at Rosemarie who had already finished
half of her green drink. The chair next to her, where Doran
was to sit, was still empty. Maybe he had the right idea.

"I wouldn't want that," Tanna said, lifting her spoon.

"Do you have a question?" Vanessa asked from her
position at the head of the table.

"I was just wondering what this is."

"It's a breakfast puree filled with all the best nutrients and excellent for digestion. Haven't you ever had it before?"

You say puree, I say gruel. "My father makes something similar with *gari*. But usually it's sweetened with—"

"I'm not a big fan of sugary foods," Vanessa smoothly interrupted. "It takes getting some used to, but your body will thank you."

"Yes, I'm sure."

"What is cari?" Raymond asked.

"It's called *gari* and it's made out of cassava. It can be made into many different things. My father likes to soak it in cold water, mix it with sugar and add evaporated milk. Sometimes my mother adds peanuts. I'd say it's lighter than your oatmeal because the *gari* tends to settle at the bottom."

"Is that what you eat for breakfast too?"

"Oh no. Tea, bread and fried eggs with plenty of fresh tomatoes, peppers and onions."

"We don't fry food here," Vanessa said. "We prefer to treat our bodies like a temple instead of a garbage dump."

"Mother!" Dillon said, just as Doran took a seat at the table. He looked much better than before, although his eyes still looked tired.

"Nice of you to join us," Vanessa said. "Your fiancée was just telling us about some of the native cooking you can expect after you're married. Be prepared to have your arteries clogged within a month."

"I know fried eggs aren't the healthiest," Tanna said. "And I try not to have that dish too often." She winked at Raymond. "Although it *is* my favorite and I like to indulge a little."

"I think you like to indulge more than a little."

Dillon started to speak, but his brother's soft tone cut him off. "Nineteen eighty-two," he said. "Would you like to share that picture?"

His mother bristled. "I burned it."

Doran grinned. "I made a copy." He rubbed his chin. "Let's see. How heavy were you at the time? Was it two hundred—"

Vanessa glared at him. "Don't you dare say another word."

He met her stare, his tone hard. "Then don't tempt me."

Vanessa lifted her green drink. "Megan made it home safely. She was happy to see you yesterday although it was brief. She hopes to see more of you today."

Tanna felt a knot form in her throat. "Megan was here?"

"Yes," Vanessa said. "Didn't Doran tell you?"

"I didn't think it was important," Doran said to his mother, his gaze fixed on Tanna.

"Men," Vanessa said with a click of her tongue. "They just don't know us very well do they?" She pinned Tanna with a significant look. "We women can't help comparing ourselves to our predecessors."

"There's no need to compare," Dillon said. "Tanna and Megan are two different women."

"Yes, very different," Vanessa said stressing the word very. "Have you met her, Tanna?"

"No," Tanna said. "I haven't had the pleasure."

"You will today. She used to have her chef cook Doran the lightest, fluffy egg white omelet. Doran used to rave about them."

"I don't rave about food," Doran said.

His mother ignored him. "Being healthy was one of the many things they had in common."

"Actually, I also believe being healthy is important," Tanna said feeling defensive. "Most times I just have jollof rice and vegetable salad."

Raymond made a face. "Rice for breakfast?"

"Oh yes. It's delicious and filling. Food doesn't care what time of day it is."

"I'd like to try it," he said, dripping some puree on his shirt.

"If you'd stop talking and focus on eating you wouldn't make a mess," Vanessa said.

Tanna grabbed a napkin and helped him clean up. "You can hardly see it," she said then noticed the wording on his oversized T-shirt. "The Quality Gentleman, huh? I'd stay away from there."

The room fell quiet.

"Why would you say that?" Vanessa asked in a neutral tone.

Tanna looked around, surprised she had such a captive audience. "My brother-in-law went there once and it was terrible. Clearly the business is poorly run."

"Poorly run you said?" Vanessa said with malicious glee.

Doran scowled. "Mom, stop it."

"No, I want to hear what your fiancée has to say. Please enlighten us"

Tanna hesitated not knowing how to interpret the tension in the room. "He said it was too noisy, probably because the walls were thin and the items were subpar. He bought a hair gel that was rancid and when he went to return it, they said there were no refunds and turned him away. I don't know what idiot is running that business, but I don't think it will be around for long."

Vanessa threw her head back and laughed uncontrollably.

Raymond, Rosemarie and Dillon continued to stare at Tanna dumbfounded.

Doran pushed back his chair and stood. "Tanna, I need to talk to you." He left the room.

She glanced around the room. Everyone avoided her gaze, except for Vanessa who looked at her one more time before laughing again. Tanna sighed then followed him.

Chapter Twenty-two

"Okay, what did I do wrong?" Tanna asked once they were alone in their bedroom.

Doran tapped his chest. "I own The Quality Gentleman."

She blinked. "No, you don't."

"Yes, I do."

"You said that your family owns Mamma Tolino's."

"My family does, but I run my own business. A business I've had for seven years. A men's grooming service."

"Called The Quality Gentleman?" she said with a groan.

He nodded, his face grim.

Embarrassment and regret made her skin burn as she realized the impact of her mistake. She'd not only insulted him *and* his business, she'd shamed him in front of his family. "Why didn't you tell me that in the beginning?" She pushed him in exasperation, but he barely moved. She was like a feather trying to fell a steel wall. She pushed him again, a little harder, still with no effect. "What is wrong with you?"

He rested his hands on his hips and looked down at where her hands had been on his chest. "Why do you keep doing that?"

Because I'm mad at you for not telling me about Megan! Why didn't you tell me she was here? That you saw her? Was she the reason you didn't come to bed last night? "Because you made a fool out of me!"

"I didn't think it mattered at the time."

"Of course it matters." She threw up one hand. "Your fiancée should at least know what the man she's going to marry does for a living! This is why we…you should have…I still hardly know you. How was I supposed to…?" Tanna briefly covered her eyes unable to gather her racing thoughts into words. "This is a nightmare."

"I'm glad you think so. You're suppose to annoy my mother, not make her happy. I can't remember the last time I heard my mother laugh."

Tanna let her hand fall and stared at him with regret. "I already apologized." She sat on the bed. "You don't have to make me feel worse." She hung her head. What could she do to fix it? Should she even try? If he was going back to Megan what his mother thought wouldn't matter anymore.

"Which location?"

Her head snapped up. "What?"

"Which Quality Gentleman did your brother-in-law go to?"

"I think it was the one in Longwood Mills."

He softly swore. "It's one of our low performing branches. What else did he notice?"

"The customer service could have been better. He said the sales associates didn't really know what they were selling."

Doran pulled out his phone. "Hey," he said once someone answered, "I need The Quality Gentleman in Longwood Mills shut down and someone there to inspect it from top to bottom. Today. No cancel that. I'll do it myself. Tell them to meet me within an hour." He disconnected.

"You can't go now," Tanna said as Doran opened the door. "The party starts in four hours."

"We'll be back by then. If not, we'll be fashionably late."

"We?"

"Yes," he said, grabbing her wrist and pulling her off of the bed. "You're going to help me."

"Absolutely not!" Vanessa said when Doran told her of his plans. "You can't rush off now."

"We'll be back in time," Doran said, leading Tanna out the front door. "It's only an hour away and I want to see for myself what's going on."

"This is why you hire people. You use them for things like this."

"People need leadership. Bye," he said, closing the door in her face.

She swung it back open. "How many times have I told you not to do that?"

Doran reached his car, quickly lifting the door handle three times before opening the door. He waved at his mother before getting in the car.

"Why do you that?" Tanna asked as she put on her seatbelt.

"Close the door in her face?" he said amused. "Because it's fun."

"No, that thing with the door handle. Is it for good luck?"

His tone changed. "I don't know what you're talking about."

"Never mind." Tanna sighed. "I know you're angry."

"I am. But I'm more angry at myself than with you. If what you're saying is true, then I've let my customers down and that's unacceptable."

"You said you started the company seven years ago?"

"Yes."

"Then why not mention anything about it? Most business owners are proud of their companies. Is it not doing well?"

"It's a success, mostly," he said not wanting to expand. He didn't want to share that not talking about his business had become a habit. Women were rarely with him for conversation and he knew his priorities. First he had his image as the family dunce to maintain, plus most people weren't impressed, especially Megan. She didn't think it was a 'sexy' sounding business and urged him to sell it and join the family company.

"What made you come up with the idea?"

He sighed, it was just like Tanna not to let a subject drop. "It's not interesting."

"That's not why I asked. I'm curious."

His father had been the first inspiration for his idea. *Presentation is powerful*, he used to say. *People are going to judge you anyway, son, you may as well direct them in the direction you want them to go.* But it was at age seven when he truly figured out what his father meant. They'd gone to the city to visit one of their father's friends. Rosemarie stayed by their father's side, while Dillon sat dutifully in one chair and read, but Doran couldn't keep still. He bounced from one chair to another, one room to the next exasperating their nanny until she told him to play a game of looking outside and counting the amount of times he saw the color red.

He didn't start the game because she told him to, he thought it would be interesting to find such a bright color in the cold, rainy day. He saw a red car, and a red sign and a red bike, he stopped when he saw a woman in a red coat, beside her stood a boy about his age. The boy appeared to be shivering and looked sad. Doran kept waiting for them to cross the street, but they never did. He called his nanny over and pointed to the pair. "Why are they just standing there?" he demanded.

"They're waiting for the bus."

"Why not get a car?"

"They may not have a car."

"Why not?"

She sighed, she was always weary of his many questions. "We've been over this."

Yes, she'd told him about poor people before, but it still bothered him. The boy shouldn't be standing out in the cold wearing an ugly jacket. Why didn't his mom buy him a good one? She looked warm, he should be warm too.

When he couldn't find his coat later that day, he didn't care that his nanny scolded him, how annoyed his father had been or upset his mother was. It didn't bother him that she called him 'her little idiot' and wished he was more like his brother.

Doran didn't care because he hadn't lost his coat. He'd asked their driver to give it to the boy.

He'd watched the driver go to the woman and boy and say something. He watched the boy put the coat on and smile. His driver pointed towards the window where Doran stood. Doran ducked out of view, his heart pounding. He didn't know why he felt suddenly shy, but he did. He didn't want to take credit. He waited a few seconds before he peeked to look outside the window again. The driver had gone and the woman and boy still stood by the corner, but they no longer looked like a sad pair standing in the rain like they had been a few moment before.

That's when his father's words stuck with him—*presentation is power.* The coat had transformed them both. The boy carried his head a little higher, his mother did too. That's when Doran knew he wanted to make others feel that way. That change didn't take much.

But he'd never shared that story with anyone and wasn't ready to now. "Men's grooming is not a new idea," he said, trying his best to sound bored about a topic he was passionate about, "just an industry I thought to expand on. A clean, well-groomed style is timeless. And I like to help men put their best foot forward and make a lasting impression. I apologize that your brother-in-law had the experience he did. If he's willing to give us another chance, I'd like to offer him the opportunity to enjoy a cool beverage in our semi private stylist's station, and give him an executive membership for one year which gives clients full access to nine haircuts, ten clean ups, and discounts on grooming services, and our retail products."

"That's very generous. I'm sure he'll jump at the chance."

"Until I get this Longwood Mills branch taken care of, I'd recommend one of our other locations."

"That would be inconvenient for him."

Doran nodded. "Fair enough… I'll have to make this branch work then and find out what's wrong."

The moment he stepped inside the facility, he knew the problems. First, the walls were too thin where the various styling stations were enclosed. The construction crew had used a lower quality material to save cost. Doran went to one of the shelves and picked up a styling gel, hoping that Tanna's brother-in-law's experience would be a rarity, but when he opened the jar the smell had his eyes watering.

"Where are you getting these products?" he asked the manager, a man who looked better fit to run a library than a grooming facility. His nose hair needed trimming, his glasses needed a good clean and his clothes were wrinkled. They met in the back of the store.

The man adjusted his glasses and swallowed. "From a supplier."

"The supplier we told you to use or one that you found on your own who would sell you items cheap so you could mark them up and make a higher profit?"

"A store like this can't do well here."

"What do you mean?"

"The clientele isn't here."

They had taken a chance with the Longwood Mills location. The average income bracket wasn't as high as the other two locations, but their market research had made it clear their target demographic was in the area. If he didn't want to only cater to men in an exclusive income bracket, he had to make the Longwood Mills branch work.

"This clientele deserves the highest quality. If you want to run a barbershop go elsewhere. My company caters to men who care about their appearance." He looked the man up and down. "Did you sleep in the store?"

"What?" the manager said, offended.

"I'm trying to figure out why your clothes are wrinkled."

The manager shrugged. "Is it really a big deal?"

"No. You can go home now. You're fired."

The man left and Doran followed him out into the main area where Tanna sat chatting with a young man, one of the sales associates, dressed in a sharp suit. When she saw Doran she said something to the young man then approached him. "How did it go?"

"I have to find a new manager."

"Good, because you're in luck."

"I am?"

She nodded. "You already have one." She nodded to the young man she'd been talking to. "I've been watching him and then asked him a few questions. He's sharp, eager and filled with ideas. He's got what it takes."

And he looked about nineteen. Would anyone take him seriously? "He's too young."

"He's not too young. He's twenty-three and it's better to promote within the ranks than bring in a newcomer. He's closer to the problems of this branch than you are and he can help you solve them."

Doran folded his arms, letting her words sink in. "You're right. Let's just hope he says yes."

They had no trouble convincing the eager sales associate to take on the new responsibilities. Doran also let him know that the business would be closed for a week for reconstruction. After discussing a few other details and listening to some of Tanna's tips for improving the overall appearance, they were ready to go.

"There's not much more you can do in one day," Tanna said to Doran once he'd finished talking to someone at the head office. "We need to get back."

"I will once I finish fixing these," Doran said, turning the bottles on the glass shelf so that the labels all faced out in a uniformed way.

"You'll likely have to throw them away and get a new batch," she said watching his meticulous care.

"Doesn't matter. I can't leave them like this."

"There are so many bottles."

"I'll be done in a minute," he said through clenched teeth, annoyed that he couldn't stop himself.

Tanna watched him, knowing it would take a lot longer than a minute to get all the bottles in order. But since it seemed important to him, she would help. However, he still had to touch whatever she'd straightened to make sure they were perfect. "Okay, now we're finished," he said.

Doran went over to a sink and washed his hands and dried them. Then he did it two more times before he headed to the car where he lifted the door handle three times before opening the door.

"Does it act up when you're upset?" Tanna asked once they'd gotten on the road.

"What?"

"Your obessive-compulsiveness?"

"I don't…it's not…you don't have to be worried about me."

"I didn't say I was worried. I'm just curious."

"I've got it under control."

"You did great back there. I know with Liam in charge of this branch it will perform just as well as your other locations."

"Hmm."

"It's okay to make mistakes."

"It shouldn't have happened."

"But it did, now let it go. I know it's hard for smart guys like you to admit, but you can't be brilliant at everything."

He turned sharply to her. "Smart?"

She held up her hands in surrender. "Why do you get upset every time I call you smart?"

He took a deep breath. "I'm not upset."

"Then stop jumping down my throat every time I say that you are. Geez, another man would take it as a compliment."

Doran tugged on his ear then said in a quiet voice, "They don't know."

"What?"

"My family doesn't think I'm smart."

Tanna stared at him for a long moment as if waiting for the punchline to a joke. "But it's obvious."

Doran shook his head. "Not to them and I've made sure to keep it that way."

"Why?"

"It was easier than…" He paused wondering why he was revealing so much. Why did he need to tell her? He'd never told anyone before. Why not just keep it to himself as he always had? But somehow he couldn't, he felt the need to share welling up inside him. He took a deep steadying breath and started again. "It's easier than trying to please them…please her."

"Oh," Tanna said, and in that one sound he heard an ocean of understanding that he'd been desperate to hear and slowly his tension disappeared. He knew she'd keep his secret and she understood why he had to.

"What gave me away?"

"I really can't believe that you've been able to fool anyone. It's as clear as glass to me, from the way you talk and look at things. I can't see you any other way."

"Give me an example," he said eager to hear her thoughts.

"You were able to walk into that place and pinpoint what was wrong down to the tiniest detail."

He shrugged. "I didn't do anything impressive. I was just following a rulebook based on the guidelines our company set. I'm an enforcer. My business partner is the brains of the operation."

"No he's not."

"What do you mean 'no he's not'?"

"Those suggestions you gave to Liam had nothing to do with a rulebook, they were on-the-spot decisions that were specific to this store. They weren't generic recommendations. You took into account the location, the clientele, the traffic and reach. You also crunched numbers at a rate that had my head spinning and I deal with numbers all day. You should stop pretending."

A devilish look came into his eyes. "Not yet. I like being my mother's disappointment. Besides, Dillon is considered the brains."

Tanna made a face. "Isn't that annoying? Don't you hate how in families everyone's allowed *one* trait? It's like we're two-dimensional cutouts. In my family I'm the smart one."

He grimaced in good humor. "And is that so bad?"

"No, but every once in a while I think it'd be fun to be the pretty one or the funny one."

Doran checked both his rearview and side mirrors then shifted lanes.

Tanna cleared her throat. "This is where you say, 'I think you're both.'"

"Both what?"

"Pretty and smart."

He pointed to himself. "I'm to say that you're pretty and smart?"

She nodded. "Yes."

"And then what do you say?"

"I say that you're both handsome and smart."

Doran checked his reflection in the rearview mirror. "Stating the obvious is easy."

"Saying you're humble would be a stretch."

He grinned. "No, it would be a lie."

She playfully patted his cheek. "Absolutely."

His grin disappeared. "But we do have a problem."

She swallowed. "What?"

"You made my mother laugh."

Tanna briefly squeezed her eyes shut. "That wasn't intentional."

"I know, but if you do it again I want a thousand dollars back."

"It won't happen again."

"And if she asks you any questions about what we were up to you'll say—"

"Doran handled it like a pro…why are you shaking your head?"

"Don't mention me, just mention the business."

Tanna rolled her eyes. "How does that make any sense? The business doesn't run itself…oh that's right, you're not supposed to be smart."

He nodded with approval. "You're catching on."

"But I don't know what to say."

"You say the Longwood Mills business had some issues that are now being addressed. You can also say that the business has a new manager and that it should be on par with the other branches soon."

"If she asks me any questions, I'll tell her to talk to . you."

"Even better."

"But you can't keep this up."

"Keep what up?"

"Pretending to be something you're not."

"Tanna, I've had a lot of practice. It's something I do." He sent her a significant look. "Why do you think I hired you?"

Chapter Twenty-three

She'd kill her mother later. If she survived dying of embarrassment.

"Are you ready yet?" Doran asked from the other side of the bathroom door.

"Almost."

She stared at her image in the full length mirror. Her mother had packed a dress from her favorite designer—a bold, red and yellow dashiki print, form fitting dress with flared waist.

She looked like a sassy Ghanaian woman. *Relax, no one will notice the difference,* a little voice said, but she'd stand out like a salmon in a school of goldfish. When she finally stepped out of the room, Doran didn't say anything about her outfit which gave her a sense of relief, but when she walked outside to join the party, all eyes turned to her.

Dillon approached her. "You look amazing."

"It is a formal occasion," Rosemarie said, "but not quite this formal."

Tanna's cheeks burned. "I know."

"Don't worry, you put us all to shame," Dillon said.

But Tanna was the one who felt like hiding. After a few minutes, Dillon and Rosemarie faded from her side as did Doran and she was left standing alone outside, trying to pretend that she belonged when she knew that she didn't. She turned to head back inside.

An older woman with green eyes and blonde highlights rushed over to her. "I love your dress. On my recent trip to Ghana I had an outfit made, but it wasn't of this quality."

"My wife was very disappointed," the man beside her said, he was of medium height with skin the color of teak.

Tanna patted the woman's hand. "I know a tailor who will come to your house, take your measurements and make you a dress that will fit you perfectly."

The woman's eyes widened. "Really?"

"Yes."

"And what material is this?"

Tanna searched her mind wishing she'd listened to her sisters when they talked fashion. "There are lots of fabric like…uh…wax, but I won't pretend to be an expert."

"What is your expertise?" the woman said with a grin.

"If you have a house you want to sell, I can showcase it to the best degree."

"Any other talents?"

"Well, since you asked…"

Vanessa stared at the scene in horror. She couldn't believe her eyes. What was Tanna doing with the Hayfields? She had no business being in their presence let alone *talking*

to them. How could this be happening? "What is that woman doing?" she said to Dillon through clenched teeth.

"A fine job of keeping your guests entertained it seems," he replied.

"I don't want her near them."

"They seem to be enjoying themselves."

"I don't care," she snapped, feeling on the verge of panic. "She's not a good representation of us and heaven knows what she's telling them. Where is your brother?"

"I don't know."

"To think he brought her here and then let her loose like this."

"She's handling herself well."

"In an outfit like that?"

"She looks beautiful. I've heard the compliments, I'm sure you have too."

Vanessa moved her shoulders with impatience. She had and they had irritated her to no end. Despite her figure and skin tone she did look fetching in the dress, but that didn't change how she felt about her. Tanna didn't belong there. Vanessa looked around the yard. "Where is he?"

"I just told you, I don't know."

"Then you take care of it." She nudged him forward when he sent her a surprised look. "Get her away from them. Now!"

"Mom—"

"Now!"

Dillon set his glass aside and approached the group. "I'm sorry," he said to the Hayfields and the two other couples that had joined them, "but I must steal her away."

"You must be the lucky one," Mr. Hayfield said holding out his hand. "Your fiancée is absolutely charming."

"Actually I'm not the lucky one, but he's around here somewhere. Excuse us," he said gently leading her away.

"Am I in trouble?" Tanna asked once they were out of hearing.

Dillon couldn't help a grin. "My mother was spitting bullets when she saw you with her prized catch."

"Will she still be spitting when they offer her foundation half a million?"

His brows shot up. "You managed that?"

Tanna flashed a smug grin. "I have my ways."

"I know why my brother fell for you."

Tanna managed a laugh. "I think you're the only one. Not even he knows that," she said, seeing Doran with Megan, declining the offering of one of the wait staff.

"Why did you take off our little disguise?"

"Disguise?"

He tapped his nose.

"Doran didn't think I needed it."

"He's right. You can't see any bruising."

"Sleep and makeup did the trick." She glanced at the couple again, her throat tightening.

Dillon caught her glance. "I saw your face when Mom mentioned Megan this morning. I want you to know that you don't have to worry about her. She's part of Doran's past."

Tanna plastered on a smile. *How little you know.* "Sure."

"What you two have together is special. Don't let anything or anyone break that."

Tanna lowered her gaze no longer able to meet his, her heart heavy and her eyes filling with tears. "You should be telling your brother this, not me." Doran was probably somewhere alone with Megan. Tomorrow they'd go their separate ways and she'd never see him again.

Dillon lifted her chin. "No, this is something you need to hear. We're not the easiest family to be a part of. I wouldn't blame you for running, but you're good for us. You're good for him and he's good for you. You make a good pair."

If only your brother thought so too. "Thanks, but I don't think I'll ever convince your mother of that."

"Give her a couple of years—"

"Decades," Tanna corrected.

"Yeah," Dillon said with a laugh. "A few decades and she'll come around."

They were laughing again. What did they find so funny? Doran thought as he watched Dillon and Tanna standing together by the lake.

"Doran, did you hear me?" Megan asked.

He nodded. "Uh huh." Sure he heard her. He heard how much she'd missed him. What a mistake she'd made letting him go. That she was glad he was happy. Words. Words. Words. She was always so good with words.

"Is it really too late for us?" she asked. "We once meant a lot to each other."

Until you fell out of love with me. "Yeah." Doran drummed his fingers against his leg, expecting a sense of victory. She wanted him back. It had been a moment he'd been waiting for. He could make her suffer a little. Let her realize what she'd lost. But the feeling of triumph didn't come.

Yesterday, she'd been his torment—flooding his heart and his mind. Today…Today he looked at her expecting his heart to still race at her gaze, the smell of her perfume to send his mind spinning. He'd prepared himself for the hurt, the sense of betrayal to renew itself, but instead he felt nothing. Instead he couldn't stop wondering why Dillon was standing so close to Tanna. And what were they talking about that made her smile like that? She looked beautiful in that dress, how come he'd never noticed before how truly beautiful she was?

"You can't keep your eyes off her." Megan followed his gaze. "You're not the man I remember, I don't think you ever looked at me that way."

That caught his attention. He turned to her. "I did, you never noticed."

"Is this for real? Your mother—"

He narrowed his eyes. "Leave my mother out of it. What do you think?"

She lightly trailed a finger down his arm. "I think that engagements can be broken."

"True."

Megan looked at Tanna again. "She's so different than me, one would think you were trying to make a point."

"And what would that point be?"

"That no one could replace me. I dated you for a year, Doran. I know what you're like. I know how you think and we both know that this woman may be fun, but she'll never be permanent and your mother will never accept her."

He folded his arms and nodded. "Tanna thinks I'm smart."

Megan blinked. "What?"

"And because she thinks I'm smart she probably wouldn't use me to negotiate a major business deal, sleep with her father's lawyer behind my back then dump me."

Color drained from her face.

Doran tapped his chin. "I bet she also wouldn't come back to me after two years when her father's company is struggling again and pretend that she loves me because she knows I'm too smart to fall for that."

Her voice trembled. "Doran, please—"

"Just as you asked me, I haven't told anyone about my role in that business deal. I'm too proud to reveal what a fool you made of me, but I won't give you that chance again."

She gripped her hands together. "Doran, you don't understand. Your mother came to me and—"

He shoved his hands in his pockets. "I don't care."

Megan held up a trembling hand. "Just listen to me."

"You think my relationship with Tanna is making a point? You're right." He leaned in close and lowered his voice. "It's that I am completely over you."

Chapter Twenty-four

W hy couldn't she fall for his brother? Tanna wondered as she fixed up her makeup in the bathroom. Dillon was handsome, considerate and he liked her. He was so sweet he almost made her cry, not the pretty tears strolling down one's face in perfect streams. The scrunch-up-your-face cry of misery. She never was a pretty crier anyway. But Dillon seemed the type who would hold her close and comfort her.

That would be something, he was as beautifully made as his brother, and though he didn't make her heart pound, perhaps he could grow on her.

Tanna put her lipstick down and shook her head. It would never work. How weird would that be to break up with one brother then end up with the other? Although stranger things have happened. But how would she explain it? Unfortunately, there was an even bigger reason it could never work—they shared the same mother. Vanessa was every girlfriend or daughter-in-law's nightmare. How had Megan managed it? Oh, right. Vanessa *liked* her. That was the difference. Doran had only chosen her because he knew his mother would feel the opposite. She had to remember that. Once the weekend was over they'd go their separate ways.

Tanna left the bathroom and was returning to the party, then stopped when she saw Raymond looking for something at the bottom of the stairs.

"There you are," Tanna said. "I'd wondered where you'd gone off to."

He jumped to his feet, his eyes wide and anxious. "I'm supposed to stay in my room. Grandma doesn't like me at her parties."

Tanna made a dismissive gesture with her hand. "It's a boring grownup party anyway. Did you drop something?"

He wrung his hands. "Sorta."

Tanna rested her hands on her hips. "Sorta isn't a word. Is the answer yes or no?"

"No, I…I lost something."

"What?"

He hesitated.

She bent down so they were at eye level. "You can tell me."

Raymond bit his lip. "I tripped against Bunny's cage and it got knocked over."

Tanna briefly closed her eyes. "Please tell me she didn't escape."

Raymond folded his arms and sighed, hanging his head.

"What color is your rabbit?"

He looked up at her. "Bunny isn't a rabbit."

Tanna tentatively licked her lips then swallowed. "What is she?"

"A white mouse."

Better than a snake, right? "You're sure she's not in your room?"

He threw up his hands. "I looked everywhere."

"It's a big house so hopefully she's still upstairs."

He swayed side to side. "If Gran finds out, I'll be in so much trouble."

"Retrace your steps."

"What?"

"Go over every step you took before you ended up here," Tanna clairfied. "I'll talk to your father."

"Do you have to tell him?" Raymond said in a tight voice. "He'll be mad too."

"Better him than your Gran."

He nodded solemnly. "You're right."

She went outside and found Dillon, who greeted her with a smile. "I just spoke to Raymond."

His smile fell. "What's wrong?"

"He accidentally knocked over Bunny's cage and she escaped."

"Dammit, I knew I shouldn't have…" Dillon briefly covered his eyes. "How long ago?"

"He's been searching for awhile. My one hope is that she stays inside and along the walls—they don't like being exposed."

"I'll check the west of the house, you check the east."

Tanna went back inside and searched the house with dread, making her way through the crowd of guests hoping not to draw too much attention to herself. The house was enormous, the mouse could be anywhere! She also couldn't call out its name even if it did respond to commands. Twice, she pretended to drop something so she could look under the chairs and tables. It was her third attempt at this pretense—she was checking under a couch—when she heard high heels stop behind her.

"What are you doing?" Vanessa asked.

Tanna scrambled to her feet. "Nothing."

"Did you lose something?"

Tanna tugged on her earlobe. "I thought I'd lost my earring, but then realized I hadn't."

A thin smile touched her lips. "How lucky."

"Yes, very," Tanna said then stopped when she saw a flash of white behind Vanessa as Bunny scurried down the hall. "Excuse me."

She followed the quick little creature then covered it with the train of her dress, before lifting it up. "Gotcha!"

"Tanna, I've been looking for you," Mrs. Hayfield said. "You were taken away and I wanted to finish our conversation."

Tanna spun around, holding her train as if she didn't want to let it drag on the ground. "Hi," she said, hoping she wouldn't lose her grip on the mouse.

"I wanted to ask where you planned to go on your honeymoon. I know a wonderful little spot in Venice that will be perfect for you and I know the owner."

"Um…we haven't thought that far." She saw Doran passing down the hallway and knew he was her only hope. "Darling?" she called out to him.

He stopped, his brows raising a fraction. "Yes?"

"Could I see you for a moment?" When Mrs. Hayfield turned to look at him, Tanna mouthed 'Help me!'

He walked over to her, his expression not revealing whether he'd seen her request or not. "What is it?"

"Mrs. Hayfield was telling me about a place in Venice for our honeymoon."

"You know I'll take you wherever you want to go," he said then kissed her on the cheek like an affectionate fiancé before lifting his lips to her ear and whispering, "What's wrong?"

"Thank you, darling," Tanna said. She smiled at Mrs. Hayfield. "He spoils me. Sometimes I feel like his favorite toy. A stuffed bunny he had as a boy. You remember that, don't you?"

He looked at her for a long moment. "My stuffed bunny?"

"Yes." She glanced down at her hand, which held her train. "Your little white *bunny*."

Understanding lit his eyes. "Yes, I loved that toy." He made a show of wrapping his arm around her waist while he covered her hand with his, Tanna loosened her grip. He grabbed the mouse then slipped it into his jacket pocket.

"We must have you both over for dinner," Mrs. Hayfield said.

"That would be wonderful," Tanna replied.

"Speaking of dinner," Vanessa's clear voice cut in. She took Mrs. Hayfield's arm and led her away. "Have you ever been to..."

Dillon came running up to them, breathless. "Any luck?"

Doran patted his pocket.

Dillon sighed in relief. "That was a close call."

"You have no idea how close," Tanna said.

Dillon smiled at her. "You saved the day. Again."

Doran frowned. "Again?"

"Yes, she's convinced the Hayfield's to invest."

"But your mother will take all the credit," Tanna said. "Not that I mind."

"You should mind." Dillon rested a hand on her shoulder, his voice as warm as his gaze. "You're a gem."

Doran handed the mouse over to his brother. "Give this to Raymond."

"I'll have to make a sturdier cage," he said, tucking the mouse away inside his jacket. "I should have kept it at home, but Raymond would have missed her." He headed for the stairs.

Tanna made a move to follow him. "At least we found him."

Doran grabbed her arm, stopping her. "Yes, I think it's time we return to the party."

Tanna looked at him surprised. "I just wanted to say a quick word to Raymond."

"You can talk to him later." He sent his brother a look. "Isn't that right?"

Dillon shook his head. "I'm not sure he'll still be up by the time the party ends."

Doran narrowed his eyes. "Then she can talk to him tomorrow."

"I'm sure you can spare her for a few minutes."

"I've spared her long enough."

Tanna waved her hand to get their attention. "I'm standing right here."

They both ignored her.

"We saw you with Megan," Dillon said. "How did it go?"

Doran gestured towards the second level. "Your son is waiting."

Dillon met his gaze in challenge, then a slow, knowing grin spread on his face. "I know," he said before heading up the stairs.

Chapter Twenty-five

"What do you mean he wouldn't listen to you?" Vanessa demanded when Megan approached her towards the end of the party. They stood alone at the lake's edge.

"He's…" Megan paused then started again. "He doesn't want to be with me."

"Of course he does. You saw how he responded to you the other day. He's just pretending can't you see that?"

"He wasn't pretending. He's over me."

"He's pouting. You have to be patient. Your part in our plan is clear."

Megan glanced towards the house. "It won't work."

"It has to work."

Megan pressed her hands together. "You don't understand—"

"I understand that we made an agreement."

"Is there another way I can—"

Vanessa blinked. "Do I look like I'm in the mood to renegotiate?"

"I know what we said, but—"

"I don't know what happened between you two, but it can be fixed. You are meant to be with my son. It was clear two years ago and it's clear now."

"Not if he's in love with another woman. I saw how he looked at Tanna."

Vanessa's lips thinned with irritation. "He's not in love with anyone. Especially *that* woman." She took control of her temper, let her mouth soften into a smile and touched Megan's cheek. "My dear, you must be strong. I told you that he would try to fight this. My son and I like our little battles, but I always win." She turned and walked away before Megan could argue.

She didn't want to fight with her, although she was beginning to make her angry. Something had shaken the young woman's confidence. Megan never used to look so defeated before. How could she wither under the weight of such a flimsy opponent? What had Doran said to her? Was Tanna truly a threat?

Vanessa stopped when she saw Tanna and Doran talking to another couple, Doran's arm casually around Tanna's waist. Had she underestimated her? She looked innocent enough, but perhaps that was how she'd been able to capture her son. Vanessa looked at Tanna closer. She'd been too subtle, she had to change tactics.

An hour later, Vanessa found Tanna standing alone on the patio watching the staff dismantle the canopy. The party had been a success, but she needed one last victory. "How much?" she said.

Tanna turned to her surprised. "I'm sorry?"

"It's not a difficult question. How much will it take to persuade you to leave my son alone?"

Tanna leaned against the railing and stared out at the lake. "Two hundred thousand should do it."

Vanessa paused, startled. Was she really that greedy? Would it all be this simple? Her heart lifted with hope. "You sound certain."

Tanna nodded, her gaze still looking out at the water. "I am. I'd been wondering how long it would take you to figure out that I'm only in it for the money." She turned to her. "I want a man I can be proud of, not some owner of men's hair salons."

Vanessa smiled at the disdain in Tanna's voice. Yes, her son's business would be an embarrassment. At least she now knew what kind of woman she was dealing with. "My son usually has better tastes."

"I picked him up when he was broken hearted. It was easy."

"I could tell him about you and not pay you a cent."

"And do you really think he'd believe you over me?" Tanna said with a laugh. "But it would be fun to see you try."

"I'll pay you in installments. I would hate to have you change your mind."

"This is non-negotiable. Everything now." A cruel smile spread on Tanna's face. "Or I become the next Mrs. Gibson."

Chapter Twenty-six

Tanna ran into her bedroom, slammed the door closed then rested against it, her heart racing. "I can't believe I just did that," she said breathless.

Doran stared at her from across the room, where he'd been looking for something in the closet. "Did what?"

"I should ask for a bonus, but I won't."

He slowly closed the closet door, his tone suspicious. "Tanna, what did you do?"

"I made your mother hate me more than you could imagine."

"How?"

"She asked me how much money I would take to leave you alone and I told her two hundred thousand. And not just that," Tanna said with a flourish. "I told her how I'd never respect a man who made his money from male hair salons, I used her terms to sound more genuine, *and* I made sure to sound really disgusted with the idea. I also told her that I was only after you for your money." She pushed herself from the door, sat on the bed and bounced on it. "Isn't that great?"

Doran ran a tired hand down his face. "I wish you hadn't done that."

"Why not?" Tanna asked, not understanding his subdued response. She thought he'd be thrilled. "It's perfect. Now when you dump me she's going to be so happy. Don't worry, I don't plan to take the money. Why are you looking at me like that? I'd thought you'd be happy. Now you can be with whomever you want." She lay back on the bed.

"And what if I want to keep seeing you?"

Tanna sat up and stared at him. "What?"

"I want to keep seeing you," he said in a deep tone.

Tanna waved her hands not daring to believe what she'd just heard. "What are you talking about? Your plan worked. We can say goodbye after this."

His dark gaze heated with longing, holding her still. "I don't want to say goodbye."

Tanna's mind raced, her body responding to the desire in his eyes. "But…but…I thought you wanted to be with Megan."

"Why would you think that?"

She rose to her feet. "B-b-because…weren't you with her last night?"

"No."

"Then where were you? Was it really work?"

Doran bit his lip. "I just…couldn't sleep."

"Were you obsessing about The Quality Gentleman? Was that it? I told you all your suggestions are great. Is the Longwood Mills location bothering you so much that you couldn't sleep?"

"No, it wasn't that."

"Then what was it?"

His eyes caught and held hers, his heated gaze getting hotter. "I wanted to sleep with you last night."

Tanna gaped at him, dazed. Was this really happening, was he really saying these words or was she dreaming? "You're not making any sense."

"I think I just made myself very clear," Doran said, closing the distance between them. "I like you." His heated gaze skimmed over her body with slow, seductive appreciation before his arms encircled her. "I want you and I want to keep seeing you."

Tanna gazed up at him, her heart singing. He wanted her. Hadn't she imagined—dreamed of him looking at her like this? Feeling his hard, hot body close to hers? He felt the same wild emotions she did and…and she'd just told his mother she'd dump him for two hundred thousand dollars! She broke free from him and stepped away, breathless with confusion and outrage. "You're telling me this now?" She pointed to the door. "I just made a complete fool of myself in front of your mother and you still want to see me?"

Doran shook his head in regret. "It wasn't supposed to happen like this."

"You think?"

He stepped towards her. "Tanna—"

She held up her hand, desperate to keep him away. If he touched her, she would crumble. "It's too late for us now. I can't fix what I've just done."

"I'll tell her the truth."

"That you paid me five thousand dollars to pretend to be in love with you and drive her up the wall?" she said in a flat tone.

"No, we'll…I'll come up with something."

Tanna sat on the edge of the bed and shook her head. "There's no way I can end up looking good after this."

Doran stood in front of her. "Yes, you can and you will. Tomorrow you'll tell her you were lying. That she made you angry and you wanted to hurt her. It's simple."

"Is it? You think it's better for me to admit that I lied to spite her? You think that will make her like me?"

He sighed, pinching the bridge of his nose. "Tanna, you can't expect her to like you."

She nodded. "I know. That's why you wanted me."

He knelt down and stared up at her. "Yes," he admitted. "But now I want you for different reasons," he said in a velvet tone, his burning gaze making his intention clear. "Reasons that have nothing to do with her or Megan or anyone. I just want to be with you." With slow deliberation he let his hands slide up her dress.

She stopped him by placing her hands over his,

although her body tingled from the contact. His hands were hot against her skin. "You're on the rebound," she said, fighting to keep her voice steady. "I told you—"

"I had rebound sex two years ago." He moved his hands from her grip and shifted them to the back of her legs. "And pity sex too." He inched his hands higher, lifting her dress. "I found a woman who pitied me and pitied me and pitied me until she couldn't pity me anymore." He pushed her dress up to her thighs.

"And she made you feel better?" Tanna said, knowing she should pull away from his gentle assault, but making no move to.

"Much better." He nudged her legs apart. "Now I'm ready to finish what we started two years ago."

"What we started?"

He looked at her, holding her gaze in a gentle challenge. "That kiss in the cottage outside your bedroom."

Tanna licked her lips, her face burning, her heart beating wildly. "You remember that?"

"Tanna," he said, his deep voice caressing her name. "I kissed you that night because I wanted to."

"I thought you were drunk."

He smiled at her innocence. "I wasn't that drunk. If your aunt hadn't arrived, I'd planned on extending our evening."

"You never mentioned it before."

He placed a kiss on her inner thigh. "I'm mentioning it now."

She swallowed, her voice barely a whisper. "I didn't say you could kiss me there."

"I know," he said kissing her other inner thigh." He lifted his gaze and held hers in a seductive challenge. "Will I get into trouble?"

Tanna could only nod, not trusting herself to speak.

He pulled down her panties. "Good because I plan to be a very bad boy," he said then disappeared underneath her dress, touching her center with his tongue.

She nearly leapt off the bed.

He came out from under her dress and stared at her, amused. "Is this your first time?"

Doing that? Yes! "No, you…just surprised me."

A rakish grin spread on his face. "Then let me surprise you some more." He eased her down on the bed, her body trembling not from fear but anticipation, his hungry dark gaze scanning her body like a burning caress. Her dress fell away and soon she lay naked in his arms. Arms that held her with a possessive fervor that aroused all her senses. With him she didn't feel 'too' anything--too fat or too smart or too dark or too foreign—she felt perfect, sublime. Wonderfully, beautifully made. She learned that she hadn't been single because there was something wrong with her, it was because she hadn't found the right man.

And the man she'd met two years ago, outside a castle one spring night, returned to her with passionate ardor, arousing an ecstasy that seemed unimaginable, but was undeniable. This time, this evening there was no plan, no pretense, no artifice. Every touch, every kiss, every gesture was real. Achingly, tenderly real.

Tanna's mind fought to question the veracity of his feelings. Was this just a moment of lust? Was he truly over Megan? But her body wouldn't let her question her own deep feelings for him. It responded to him like a boat seeking the beacon of a lighthouse. His silent, consistent demands called her to him with a power she could not refuse. Because she knew as he explored every part of her that she wasn't surrendering to him because he was handsome or rich or smart. She was surrendering to the man she'd been searching for. And when he entered her and their bodies became one in one perfect rhythmic motion she felt as if she'd shatter into a million pieces.

She expected to wake up from a dream. To feel the whack of her Aunt Violet's hand against the back of her head. It never came. Instead, Tanna lay in the shelter of Doran's sleeping embrace, in a daze. It had all happened so fast. Only yesterday, no only a few hours ago, it had all been make believe and now…now their relationship was real. Was this real? Would she wake up from this dream? Or was it really a nightmare? She loved him. She'd made that mistake already. She'd fallen for him even though she shouldn't, but she couldn't stay. She couldn't hold onto him. What they had couldn't last. They'd both been driven by a primal need, but she had to be rational.

Tanna let her gaze look around the room. They hadn't even turned the lights off. She wouldn't have to grope around in the dark as she gathered her things. Now all she needed to do was slip out of bed unnoticed. She shifted to the side.

Doran tightened his hold around her waist, and pulled her closer. "Where are you going?" he mumbled.

"To the bathroom."

"I don't believe you."

"After the bathroom I was going to slip away and disappear," she confessed.

"I know where you live," he said with a chuckle.

"That's true but at least I'd be in my territory."

He loosened his hold. "You really want to leave me?"

"No," Tanna said, turning to face him, joy and misery shining in her eyes. "I want to stay with you, but if I stay I'm going to get hurt. Now your mother's opinion will matter. Before I could laugh away her cruel words, now…" She shook her head. "You don't understand."

"I do understand," he said with feeling. "I know how much her words hurt. I've pretended my whole life that I didn't care, but every time she gets me, just a little, even though I've learned never to let it show."

"I'm not as strong as you."

He tenderly cupped her cheek, his voice low, insistent. "I'll protect you."

She pressed her cheek against his hand, feeling his strength, but still afraid. "You can't protect me from her."

His eyes darkened dangerously. "You don't trust me?"

"I didn't say that."

He let his hand fall. "After we leave here, you won't have to see her again."

"You can't promise that."

"The only opinion that matters right now is mine. She'll come around."

"And if she doesn't?"

"She will. Forever's a long time."

"You think we'll be together forever?" Tanna said with a laugh.

"Are you planning on marrying somebody else?"

Her laughter died on her lips. She stared at him stunned. "You're asking me to *marry* you?"

He nodded, his gaze suddenly shuttered.

Tanna covered her face with the sheets and groaned.

Doran pulled the sheets away, amusement in his eyes. "What is it?"

Tanna pulled the sheets back up over her face. "I won't be able to sleep now."

"Why not?"

"The thought of Vanessa as my mother-in-law will give me nightmares."

Doran tugged the sheets down again. "But you'll have me. And you like Rosemarie and Raymond."

"Yes," she said, suddenly thoughtful, a slow smile touching her lips. "And Dillon as a brother-in-law won't be too bad either."

Doran frowned. "I'm not enough?"

She playfully trailed her fingers down the length of him before patting his chest. "Oh, you're definitely more than enough. But when it comes to offers of marriage, a woman's got to take her time."

Chapter Twenty-seven

She hadn't said 'yes'. Doran stood on the patio the next morning, a fresh breeze rising off of the lake. He barely noticed it as he leaned against the railing. He'd left Tanna alone still asleep. He'd thought of waking her so that they could enjoy breakfast in bed, but then rejected the thought. They weren't newlyweds yet. In truth they weren't really anything. He knew she liked him and last night she'd shown him how much. His body could still remember the trail of her fingers down his back, the feel of her legs wrapped around him, the hot liquid fire that invited him inside.

But she hadn't said 'yes'. She hadn't said 'no' either, but she certainly hadn't said 'yes' and Doran wasn't sure how long he could wait for her answer. He hadn't meant to ask her to marry him last night. It had been impulsive, reckless. He prided himself on being smarter than that, but once he'd said the words he didn't want to take them back. He wanted to hear her answer. His heart pounding out every second. She was the one for him. He didn't want to lose her. But did she feel the same? Was a lifetime out of the question?

Doran gripped the railing, suddenly feeling sick. She meant too much to him; what she thought mattered so much it made him weak. He had to let her go. He had to make himself not care, that was his only defense. She couldn't be this important to him.

But dammit she was. He couldn't imagine his life without her.

But he should have taken his time. He should have waited until he knew she was sure about him, before making his move. He'd made a fool of himself with Megan and he'd waited a year. How could he have said what he did? Why was his heart so eager to make a fool of him again? Maybe he should tell her that marriage was something he was thinking about for the future. That there was no pressure for her to answer him now. She was right, he had to give her time to adjust to the thought of being part of his family. He couldn't blame her for wanting to run away. He had to be patient.

Doran pushed himself from the railing. Once he got Tanna away from this place, he'd work on making her forget his mother and focus only on being with him.

He walked back inside and headed for the stairs.

"Have you seen Mom?" Dillon asked him from the landing.

"No."

"Nobody has."

"Nobody has what?" Rosemarie asked coming out of her room.

"Seen Mom."

"I last saw her around the back."

"When was that?"

"Last night."

Dillon sighed. "That doesn't help. Nobody has seen her all morning."

"She's not in her room?" Rosemarie asked. "Maybe she's sleeping late."

Dillon slapped his forehead. "Now why didn't I think of that?" he said his tone dripping with sarcasm. "She's probably tucked away in a bed that hasn't been slept in."

"You don't need to be rude," Rosemarie said. "And you hadn't mentioned her bed not being slept in."

Doran shoved his hands in his pockets and rocked back on his heels. "She probably went out and didn't tell anyone."

"Her car's still here," Dillon said. "I've called her cell phone and it goes directly to voicemail."

"What's going on?" Tanna asked, joining them.

"Mom's missing," Dillon said.

Rosemarie shook her head. "We don't know if she's missing."

"But we don't know where she is."

"I'm sure she'll show up soon," Doran said. "Don't worry."

"When did you last see her?" Dillon asked.

Doran shrugged. "At the party."

Dillon looked at Tanna.

She hesitated remembering their awful conversation. "I saw her on the patio."

"When?"

"Around eleven, I think. I didn't do anything to her," she said, feeling guilty about how she'd spoken to her.

Dillon sent her an odd look. "I didn't say you did."

"Not that we would blame you," Rosemarie added.

"How did she seem?" Dillon said insistent.

Tanna looked at Doran for help. She didn't want to have to share what had happened between her and his mother. He stepped forward. "Mom's a grown woman. She went somewhere to be alone. When she gets back, tell her we said goodbye."

"You're leaving?" Dillon asked surprised.

"We only planned to stay for the weekend."

"But Mom—"

"She's probably doing this to annoy us. Remember that time when she was mad with Dad and disappeared for three days?"

"That was a long time ago."

"She's still the same person."

Rosemarie held up her hands. "We're too close to the situation. Let's get an outsider's opinion." She looked at Tanna. "What do you think? Should we worry like Dillon or ignore it like Doran?"

Tanna paused, her gaze darting between the two brothers. She felt as if she were making more than a choice of who to believe. "Um…I think Doran has a point."

Dillon hung his head; Doran smiled.

"Okay," Rosemarie said. "Then we'll wait and see."

"Maybe we should have stayed a little longer and waited for her to return," Tanna said as Doran drove her back home.

He looked at her surprised. "Consider yourself lucky. Do you really want to face her again after last night?"

"No, but your brother looked really worried."

"Dillon finds reasons to worry. Mom's fine. She's probably still fuming about the money you asked for. I wouldn't put it past her to disappear for a few hours or even a couple of days just to annoy me. She'll show up."

But she didn't.

Three days later and nobody had heard from or seen Vanessa Gibson. By the fourth day Doran and Tanna were back at the lake house with Dillon and Rosemarie.

"For the sake of the business we have to keep this a hushed matter," Dillon said as he tended to a bruise on Raymond's face. His son had stepped on a rake in the shed and given himself a huge bruise on the forehead. The rest of the adults sat around the dining room table, the summer afternoon casting hushed rays of light onto the wooden table, dancing off of the chandelier. "I'll go to the police and make sure it's handled with the utmost discretion."

"You could have told us this over the phone," Doran said.

"I think it's important we're all here to talk to the police."

"There's been no ransom demand, so I think—"

"Nobody cares what you think, Doran," Rosemarie snapped. "We listened to you the first time and look what happened."

Doran tapped his chest. "You're saying this is my fault?"

"No, but this is important. We need to follow what Dillon says and not argue with him. This is critical. Do you know what would happen if word gets out that the head of Mamma Tolino's is missing? I know you don't care about the family business, but it's important to us."

"I didn't say it wasn't. I just—"

"Thought she'd come back. Well she didn't. You were wrong, but it was our fault for listening."

"This isn't anybody's fault," Tanna said trying to ease the tension in the room. "And pointing fingers isn't going to help us find Vanessa."

"You're all done," Dillon said to his son. "Go upstairs and play."

"Will Gran be all right?" Raymond asked.

"We hope so." He patted him on the bottom. "Now go." He waited for his son to leave the room then said, "Tanna's right. We need to be clear headed and remember as much as we can about that night. We've already lost a lot of time. Are we agreed? We talk to the police?"

They nodded.

Soon they were at the police station sharing the information they had, moments later the police were talking to the house staff and contacting those who had attended the party and quickly determined one important fact: Tanna was the last person to see Vanessa before she disappeared.

Chapter Twenty-eight

She'd lied to the police.

Tanna wrung her hands as she stared out the sitting room window, fireflies dotting the evening. She couldn't believe she'd lied to the police. She hadn't told them the real topic of her conversation with Vanessa. She hadn't told them how much the older woman couldn't stand her, how angry Vanessa had been when she left her on the patio. If she told them the truth, would they think she'd done something to her? How would it make her look in their eyes if she told them she'd tried to get money from her?

"You barely ate anything at dinner," Doran said, coming up behind her.

"I'm going to go to jail," Tanna said in a low voice.

"What?"

She turned to look at him. "I'm going to jail."

He looked around to make sure nobody had overheard her then said quietly, "No, you're not."

"I lied to the police. I didn't tell them what I said to her."

"You didn't have to. That information wouldn't help the investigation."

"How do you know that?"

"What you said has nothing to do with her disappearance."

"You don't know that either. What if she got so upset she…"

"Killed herself?" Doran said with a cruel laugh. "Don't be so dramatic. My mother certainly isn't. Besides, if she had, she would have left instructions for her funeral."

Tanna hugged herself. "That isn't funny."

"I'm not being funny. I'm serious. I know my mother and she wouldn't kill herself without leaving a note and instructions. Vanessa Gibson is not a woman to leave without a trace."

But she had. "What should I do if the police find out the truth?"

"How would they find out? Nobody else was there." He cupped her chin tenderly, his hand warm. "You're not a suspect, Tanna." He let his hand fall as well as his gaze. "If anyone's to blame, it's me." He turned to the window. "I took her disappearance too lightly. We should have searched sooner."

Tanna gently tugged on his sleeve. "You wouldn't have known."

"It was a stupid mistake."

"But a mistake all the same. It happens."

He shook his head, his voice harsh. "It shouldn't have. She could be in real trouble."

"The police will find her."

"And if she's hurt or dead, I'll have that on my conscience forever," he said through clenched teeth. "Rosemarie and Dillon will never let me forget it."

"She may be alive and just lost. We don't know anything." Tanna took his hand. "But I do know one thing, no matter what happens, my answer is yes."

Doran sharply turned to her.

Tanna nodded at the disbelief in his eyes and smiled.

Doran didn't move. He stood frozen, as if afraid the moment would disappear. She'd said yes. She'd marry him. Even after all he'd put her through. He thought he might have lost her this afternoon. His mind still burned at the memory of the doorknob to the front of the house.

They'd planned to leave the house to talk to the police. Dillon and Rosemarie had gone ahead of them.

"What?" he'd asked Tanna, who stared up at him from the bottom of the front steps.

"You just checked the door five times."

He shrugged wanting to appear nonchalant although inside he was in turmoil. "I just want to make sure it's locked," he said checking it again. He took a few steps then knew he had to go back. "Get in the car, I'll be right there."

She folded her arms. "I can wait."

He checked a seventh time. Then an eighth. "I said I'll meet you in the car," he said, wishing she'd go. Wishing she'd turn away so she wouldn't see him.

He was in a loop and he knew it. He couldn't get away from the door. Every time he checked, he had to check again. And again. It wasn't right. He knew it didn't make sense. He knew the door was closed, the house locked. But he couldn't get away. But something kept drawing him back. He knew it was crazy, he knew he *looked* crazy, but he couldn't escape it. He'd once had to miss a dinner date because he had to keep checking the oven was off.

Tanna held out her hand. "Give me the key."

"Why?"

"Because I need to get something inside. You wait by the car."

"Okay," he said, relieved to release the keys to her.

She went inside and came out a few moments later. "I told you to wait by the car," she said when she still saw him standing where she had left him. "I'll lock up."

Doran turned and went to the car, his hands in his pockets. Right, if she locked up then he didn't have to worry anymore. The loop was broken.

She unlocked the car. "Do you want me to drive?"

"I can drive," he snapped, embarrassment making his words harsh.

She handed him the keys and got inside.

He started the engine the put the car into reverse. "I'm sorry."

But the day didn't get any better, once they reached the police station he got out of the car and locked it. Then checked that it was locked three times.

Tanna held out her hand. "Give me the keys."

"I'm fine, just go inside and I'll be there."

"Doran."

"I'm just...checking..." He knew he was being irrational, but couldn't seem to stop. His sight and touch told him the car was locked, but another insistent voice told him it wasn't and if it wasn't, the car could get stolen or...

Tanna's voice broke through his thoughts. "Let's go for a drive."

"We just got here."

"But you're not ready."

"I'm fine."

"You're not fine."

"I'm not crazy either."

"I didn't say you were."

"I just need to do this a couple more times and—what!" He cried when she snatched the keys from him.

"We're going for a walk."

"I didn't come here to walk, I came here to find out—"

"How can you find out anything when you're wound so tight you can hardly function?"

She was right, and her words hurt, but he was too proud to admit it.

Tanna walked towards the main road forcing him to follow her, which he did with reluctance. But soon her silent, steady walk calmed him. He'd expected her to ask questions or offer advice like most people did. Have you thought of medicine? Therapy? How long have you had this problem? Have you thought of deep breathing? But she stayed quiet by his side and he took a deep breath, feeling as if he could breathe again. The irrational impulses waning. He thought of Megan and her disgust of his 'eccentricities'. Was that the reason she'd fallen out of love with him?

He'd gotten better, but he hadn't conquered it and his mother's disappearance had only made the impulses grow, giving him a false sense of control. "This is why I'm not part of the business," he finally said the sound of a motor-cycle's engine roaring down the street drowning out his words.

"What?"

He took a deep breath, resisting the urge to pretend he hadn't said anything. "I said…this is why I'm not part of the business. I had a major meltdown and let's just say I haven't wanted to repeat it."

She nodded and again surprised him by not speaking and he felt more of his tension ebb. She stared at him as if nothing had changed, as if he were an ordinary man.

And now she stared at him in that same accepting away except she'd given him an answer that had made his heart jump. No matter what, she'd be his.

In one forward motion she was in his arms, his mouth covering hers with a passion that left her breathless. And for a brief moment their world of troubles washed away as they held onto each other as if their love could shelter them from heartbreak.

A few feet away Rosemarie watched them in amazement. She'd only heard the ending part of their conversation and had stopped to eavesdrop and see how they acted when they were alone. She expected to see the ridiculous glances and kisses gone, replaced with the cool detachment of two people trying to pull a con. But she'd been surprised to see that nothing had changed. That the looks and touches they gave to each other seemed even more ardent and real than when they were in public. The way her brother looked at Tanna seemed even more devoted than it had been only two days ago. Had Doran been telling them the truth all along? Had he really found the woman he'd planned to marry?

When Rosemarie saw them embrace, her stomach dropped as the sight of them gave answer to her question. She had to face the truth and its consequences.

Chapter Twenty-nine

Dillon found his sister in the kitchen, sitting at the empty table with her head buried in her hands. He'd already spent ten minutes trying to assure his son that the world wasn't coming to an end because his grandmother was missing and now his sister was falling apart on him. He walked over to her, resting a tender hand on her shoulder. It wasn't like her to break down, but the strain of the unknown was getting to all of them. "It's going to be all right," he said. "We'll find her."

Rosemarie let her hands fall to the table with a thud and shook her head. "That's not what's bothering me. I can't believe you were right."

Dillon took a seat in front of her, confused. "Right about what?"

"I just saw Tanna and Doran alone together." She covered her face again and groaned.

"So what?"

She mumbled something.

He leaned in closer. "What did you say?"

She looked at him. "I said it's real. They're really engaged. They're really in love."

Dillon couldn't stop a smile, happy for some good news. He'd won the bet. "Fortunately, you can write me a check."

He couldn't sleep. Doran stood on the pier and stared into the lakes dark waters, the evening warm although his body felt cold. *Where was she?* There had been no reports of accidents, hospital visits or unclaimed bodies at the morgue, for which he was thankful, but it didn't ease his concern. His mother had to be somewhere. The police had pinpointed her to one location, but she'd been moved—why or by whom they didn't know. They felt as if they'd missed her only by a couple of hours. They believed she was still alive, but there were still more questions than answers. He took a deep breath and inhaled the light scent of perfume. A fragrance that was familiar, but not his mother's.

"I was going to call," a female voice said behind him, "but I thought I'd find you here."

He spun around and saw Megan coming towards him, her heels tapping against the wooden boards. "What are you doing here?"

"I had to see you."

"That's not a good idea," he said ready to walk past her.

"Please, don't," she said desperate. "I need your help."

His brows shot up. "My help? At a time like this? My mother—"

"I know. I've done something awful and I don't know what to do," she said in a choked voice. "You're the only person I could think of to help me."

Doran paused. He knew that look, that tone…it wasn't good. "Megan, what did you *do*?"

She held the side of her head and closed her eyes. "She drove me to it. I just couldn't get her to stop."

"My mother?"

She nodded.

"Tell me what happened," he said in a gentle tone.

She let her hands fall and met his eyes. "She was black-mailing me. She promised to help bailout my father's company if you and I got back together. You know how much my father's company means to me."

"Yes," he said in a grim tone.

"I was desperate. Losing his business will kill my father, I had to do something and I thought it would work. I do like you Doran and we do—did—make a good match."

He folded his arms. "You're starting to lose my sympathy. Tell me what happened next."

Megan tucked a strand of hair behind her ear with a trembling hand. "The night of the party she called me in a rage telling me that I had to get you away from Tanna. That she was a gold digger. I told her that there was nothing I could do. That's when she said she knew about Adam."

"What about him?"

"Somehow she found out he was stealing from the business. She threatened to expose everything."

"You're still in love with him," Doran guessed in a flat tone. "And had to protect him."

She nodded, looking miserable. "I couldn't let your mom hurt my father *and* him so I…snapped."

Doran rested his hands on his hips, beginning to lose patience. "What did you do?"

"I met her over there," she said, pointing to the wooded path, "and…and knocked her out. Adam helped me move her to a secret location. I thought I could convince her to change her mind—"

"But she won't," Doran finished, knowing how his mother would act.

"I thought if we let her suffer a little with no food or water she'd come around, but she kept making threats and Adam…I think Adam's ready to do something drastic. So I moved her and hid her from him." She stepped towards him, a tremor touching her lips. "Now I don't know what to do next. You've got to help me. I never meant for it to come to this."

She wanted his help? They'd kidnapped his mother and she wanted *him* to help *them*? An image of them kissing, touching, laughing in the castle hallway flashed in his mind. He remembered the pain of their betrayal. He could get his revenge now. He could have them charged and put away, but he wouldn't. He didn't need revenge. He'd already proven he was the better man, he knew his life was better without her.

He needed to use the situation and turn it in his favor. But first he needed to know one thing. "Where is she?"

Chapter Thirty

She was alive! Vanessa slowly opened her eyes, feeling the soft touch of the hospital pillow under her cheek, the hard surface of a mattress beneath her. She hadn't thought anyone would find her. From what she'd overheard from the nurses, she'd been severely dehydrated and close to death. That witch had nearly killed her! She would get back at Megan and that man of hers, but first she had to regain her strength. Every part of her body hurt. She would have to request better sheets. These were too scratchy against her skin. And she'd want her bed moved so that she could face the window at a better angle.

Vanessa's gaze moved from the window to the figure sitting near her head. Her heart lifted at the sight of her son. Her dear boy Dillon who was her pride. The one she could always depend on; who always did what he was told. Too bad he'd had such a disastrous marriage and useless son, but that wasn't his fault, poor thing. She would make sure he found a new wife. She lifted her gaze to meet his eyes and her joy dimmed. It wasn't Dillon, it was the other one.

The other one who'd found her. She'd overheard that too. How he'd called the ambulance after finding her, why did he have to be her rescuer?

"It's too late, Mom," Doran said with heavy irony. "I know you're awake."

Maybe if she pretended to have a headache…

"I'm not going anywhere," Doran said as if reading her mind. "We need to talk."

Wouldn't he give a sick woman some space?

"Tanna told me about the bribe."

Damn. "Did she tell you what she said?"

"Of course. She wanted to see what you would do."

"She called your business 'hair salons.'"

He nodded undisturbed. "Mimicking you exactly."

"I will never accept her."

"Yes, you will."

"I may have been wrong about Megan and once I'm through with her and her family--"

"You're not pressing charges."

"What?" Vanessa said on the verge of a laugh. He couldn't be serious.

"Megan tried to protect you. She was worried Adam might harm you so she moved you from the boathouse where they'd kept you, to the crawlspace underneath the porch of the house across the lake."

"The one for sale?"

He nodded.

"And I'm supposed to be grateful for that? That she had be tied, gagged and dragged like a sack of flour?"

He shook his head. "I didn't say you needed to be grateful, only that you're not pressing charges."

"What?"

"Did you lose your hearing while being kept underneath the porch?"

Vanessa reached for the call button. "Go. I'm getting a nurse."

Doran moved it out of reach. "You're not pressing charges and I'll tell you why."

Vanessa laughed even though it hurt. "Look at you trying to stand up to me. Do you think any other mother would deal with your failings as graciously as I have?"

"There's no reason to bring that up," Doran said in a soft voice. "That was seven years ago."

"It could have been seventeen years. It was a moment I'll never forget. How could I forget the day my son made a laughing stock out of me? Everybody saw you have a meltdown, opening and closing a door nearly twenty times!"

"I've gotten better—"

"But you're not cured and do you know why? Because you're stupid and you're weak. How I abhor a weak man. And now you're trying to use my vulnerable state against me and tell me what to do. It won't work. I will press charges because I do what *I* want to. And you will not marry Tanna because if you do, you'll regret it."

"Mom," he said with a patience she'd never heard before. "I'm not here to convince you of anything. I'm here to see you one last time."

She paused. "What?"

"I'm saying goodbye. Once I walk out that door I'm never going to see you again."

Panic gripped her. Was he serious? He couldn't mean it. He would choose that woman over her? "You can't do that. I'm your mother. After all I've given you and sacrificed—"

"You haven't sacrificed a thing." He stood and squeezed her arm. "Bye," he said then turned.

"Wait!"

He spun around, his eyes blazing with controlled rage. "Why should I wait? Why should I wait to walk out that door and finally be completely happy? Why should I wait to spend my life with a woman who doesn't see me as stupid and weak?" He pointed to the exit. "Outside that door is the woman I love and the life I want. I have nothing left here."

"Doran, families always have their differences. But we stay together no matter what."

Doran shook his head. "The price for staying in this family is too high…unless you're willing to make a few concessions."

She blinked, stunned. "Me?"

He nodded.

Vanessa bit her lip conflicted. He was winning this round and she didn't know how to outmaneuver him. He was not the man she knew, there was a new fire in his eyes, a new confidence in his stance. Was Tanna the reason for it? She had been wrong about Megan. Dreadfully wrong, but it galled her to think that Tanna could be the right choice. "I'll listen, but that doesn't mean I'll accept."

"Fair enough." He sat back down next to her bed, a glint of humor in his gaze and she realized he'd made her do exactly what he wanted. "First, you're not going to press charges." He held up his hand before she could speak. "Unless you're willing to publicly admit to blackmail. Remember you have a reputation to maintain. You leave their punishment to me. Agreed?"

"I have to think about it."

He glanced at the clock. "This offer lasts about thirty seconds."

"I want to—"

"Twenty-five."

"All right. You handle them, but I want to know every-thing."

"You will."

Vanessa shifted in her bed. When had he gotten so sharp and savvy? She used to run circles around him. "Is that all?"

"Of course not. You will accept Tanna. You don't have to like her, but you will treat her cordially."

"And if I don't?"

His tone turned to ice. "Try me. I'm only giving you one chance."

She sighed, then shrugged her shoulders with impatience. "I don't have a choice, do I?"

"Not if you want to see me again."

"I don't even know why I do."

He kissed her on the cheek. "Because you love me."

She frowned. "You're so irritating."

But he was right, she did love him. While trapped and starved she'd been forced to think about her priorities and she'd prayed and hoped to see her family again. She realized how much they meant to her—even him. The one who'd fought with her, pushed her all of his life. And for the first time, as she looked at him, she didn't see a naughty boy or a rebellious teen, she saw a man. A man with a life she couldn't try to control anymore.

"Can I call her by a different name?" Vanessa asked as Doran walked to the door.

"No. By the way, there's something else you need to know about Tanna."

"What is it?"

"She can tell us apart."

Vanessa silently moaned, remembering the proverb that had been handed down to every twin in her family line for generations *Marry the one who can tell you apart, for they're the one to hold your heart.*

Her defeat was now undeniable. "Will you at least get married in the family church? I'm not interested in any native rituals she may have in mind."

"We'll think about it."

Doran left his mother's hospital room with a smile and found Tanna in the hallway, her eyes wide with worry.

He took her hand, giving it an affectionate squeeze, unafraid of how much he loved her. There were few things he was afraid of anymore. He looked at the earrings that glittered in her ears, he'd had them designed to match the family ring he'd given her to make their engagement official and she had worn them everywhere. He kissed her on the forehead, not trusting himself to kiss her anywhere else. He looked forward to getting her alone where he didn't have to behave himself. "It's all right. She's agreed to everything."

"Did you tell her about Megan and Adam?"

He'd tell her what he'd done after she was discharged from the hospital. In the three days his mother had been in the hospital, Megan's father had been forced to file for bankruptcy and as his daughter had feared, he'd suffered an attack and presently was in a rehabilitation center. Adam immediately showed his true nature. He disappeared, leaving Megan to deal with the collapse of her father and his business all alone. He didn't want his mother's accusations to compound her grief. She'd been punished enough. "No, not yet. I'll wait for her to be stronger."

Tanna nodded. "You're right. Now we just have one more problem."

His good mood fell. "What?"

"Aunt Violet."

Fortunately, she wasn't as adamantly against the match as his mother had been, although she hadn't trusted his intentions were pure until she saw him on their wedding day. It was a lavish ceremony that mixed both cultures. The bride wore a white gown and the groom a tux while her family and friends wore blue and silver *aso-ebi*. Bright pink and white roses burst from glass centerpieces vases accented by cowrie shells.

Tantoluwa "Tanna" Joelle Ariyo felt like a queen as she said her vows and exchanged rings with Doran Keenan Gibson, the man who'd stolen her heart. She briefly looked out at the crowd and saw Ambrosia with tears in her eyes, Hallie sitting next to her, no longer looking as fatigued as she had been. She had been diagnosed with malnutrition due to her finicky eating habits. She was on a new diet and her inflamed joints were healing.

Her gaze shifted to Raymond's beaming face, a bandage over his eye; he'd gotten hit with a ball while playing tennis. She saw her sisters holding a box of tissues between them and Rosemarie looking as if she still couldn't believe the ceremony was really happening. Tanna then looked up at

Doran feeling a bottomless joy she couldn't describe, unable to believe she'd been so miserable only two years ago.

At the reception, a woman Tanna knew by sight but not by name, with rust blonde curls and well endowed measurements, rushed over to her after she and Daron had finished their first dance as husband and wife. "You two make such a lovely couple," the woman said. She squinted her eyes and pointed at Doran. "And I know I've seen him before."

Doran grinned. "Yes, you have."

She clapped her hands together pleased. "I knew it. I never forget a face. Tanna, where did you find this handsome man?"

Doran and Tanna shared a private look before Tanna said, "At a wedding…"

About the Author

Dara Girard is an award-winning, national bestselling author of more than thirty books including *Just One Look*, *The Amber Stone* and *Dangerous Curves*. Dara loves to travel and hear from readers.

You can write her at:
contactdara@daragirard.com
or
P.O. Box 10345
Silver Spring, MD 20914

If you'd like to receive a reply, please send a self-addressed stamped envelope. Visit daragirard.com to join her newsletter and be the first to find out about current and upcoming releases.